IN THE NAME OF JUSTICE

When a lawman goes bad, it seems things can only end one way. For once-respected marshal and bounty hunter Laredo Judson, it looks likely to end with a hanging. But then the mysterious Miriam Hargrove offers him a deal — his freedom in return for his unique abilities as a man-hunter. His target: the cold-blooded Carson Nix. Laredo doesn't have much choice in the matter; not if he wants to go on breathing. So he takes the deal, straps on his gun and hits the trail. . .

STEVE HAYES

IN THE
NAME OF
JUSTICE

Complete and Unabridged

LINFORD
Leicester

First published in Great Britain in 2015

First Linford Edition
published 2016

A catalogue record for this book is available
from the British Library.

ISBN 978–1–4448–2934–1

Published by
F. A. Thorpe (Publishing)
Anstey, Leicestershire

Set by Words & Graphics Ltd.
Anstey, Leicestershire
Printed and bound in Great Britain by
T. J. International Ltd., Padstow, Cornwall

This book is printed on acid-free paper

For the Mex

1

The guards at Huntsville Prison, Texas, escorted their prisoner from his cell on Death Row out into the walled yard where the gallows stood grimly silent in the pale early-morning light.

The prisoner, former lawman and feared bounty hunter Laredo Judson, shuffled between the guards, his wrist- and leg-irons clanking with each step. Tall and sinewy, with cat-quick reflexes, he stared straight ahead, his rugged, jut-jawed face expressionless so that neither the warden nor the awaiting hangman could tell what he was thinking.

That is, unless they had looked into his deep-set, cold gray eyes. Then they would have seen the deep-rooted rage that had been there ever since Laredo came home one morning to discover that outlaws had torched his cabin.

Worse, inside were the charred bodies of his beloved wife and teenage daughter. Torn and bloodied pieces of their clothing that had survived the flames implied that both women had been beaten and raped and left to die in the fire.

The horrific tragedy forever changed an honorable, much-admired town sheriff into a merciless, vengeful bounty hunter who always brought in the bodies of outlaws he caught tied face-down over their saddle. It was rumored that many of them had tried to surrender. It didn't matter: Laredo ignored their pleas and shot them anyway. And when questioned about his ruthless methods, his answer was always the same: He'd been forced to kill them because they tried to escape. And since there weren't any witnesses and his prisoners were dead, no one could prove if Laredo was telling the truth or had shot them without provocation.

His brutal, cold-blooded killings disturbed many law-abiding citizens over the years. But his long, unblemished record of always getting his man kept his critics at bay, enabling him to get away with legalized murder.

Then, two months ago in Houston, Laredo made a mistake. During a gunfight between himself and three outlaws he was pursuing, he had accidently killed an innocent bystander. If the victim had been an ordinary citizen, Laredo probably would have been exonerated of all criminal charges. But the young man he shot was the only son of Texas Governor Noah Reed, and Laredo was arrested. Genuinely remorseful, he expected some type of punishment — time in jail, possibly even a short prison sentence — but certainly not a rope.

However, bullying pressure by the notoriously vindictive, grieving Governor forced the prosecutor and the jurors to ignore the eye-witnesses' statements, and Laredo was found guilty of murder and sentenced to hang.

His attorney begged him to appeal the verdict, claiming that he was sure he could get Laredo's death sentence reduced to life imprisonment. But Laredo, knowing how much the Governor hated him and how influential he was in the state, knew they would never find an impartial judge or jury, and refused to appeal.

As a result, on this fateful mid-July morning of 1888, Laredo climbed the gallows' steps and stood quietly as the hangman put a black hood over his head, looped the noose around his neck, tightened the knot and grasped the lever that sprung the trapdoor under his feet.

Warden Drake cleared his throat. 'Does the prisoner have any last words?'

'Yeah,' Laredo growled. 'I hope all you miserable bastards rot in hell!'

Unperturbed, the warden nodded to the hangman, who pulled the lever, springing the trapdoor.

2

Laredo dropped through the opening, expecting to die. But instead of the noose strangling him and the hangman's knot breaking his neck, the rope came loose from the crossbeam and Laredo landed in a crumpled heap on the ground.

Shaken and confused, he lay there a moment, trying to grasp what had happened. Then hands grabbed him and dragged him from under the gallows. A moment later, one of the guards barked: 'C'mon, damn you, stand up!'

More hands jerked him roughly to his feet and led him stumbling, leg-irons clanking, back into the prison. Once inside, the noose and hood were removed. Squinting as the light hit his eyes, Laredo saw that he was in the stone-walled corridor leading to the chapel and the padre's quarters. He had countless questions. But before he could say anything the guards led him into the candlelit chapel, where earlier he'd refused to accept religious comfort from the priest, and made him sit in a back-row pew. He tried to look around, but a guard clubbed him across the head and told him not to move!

After a few minutes, the chapel door opened and closed and footsteps approached. A woman's voice ordered the guards to step back. As they obeyed, the woman sat in the pew in front of Laredo, turned and faced him.

One look at her convinced him that here was the most confident, self-assured woman he'd ever met — *and* the unhappiest. Dressed in a stylish black frock coat and a white blouse fastened at her throat, she had sun-colored hair pulled back in a bun, a stern but attractive face with dark unforgiving eyes, a chiseled nose and jaw, and a tight-lipped mouth that had forgotten how to smile.

'Water?' she asked without introducing herself.

When he nodded, she motioned to the tallest of her three special deputies who hovered nearby. All were young muscular men dressed in gray western-style suits, white shirts and black string ties. All were bareheaded and had their heads shaved. All carried double-barreled shotguns. And all possessed the cold, dark, merciless eyes of executioners.

The tall deputy handed the woman a canteen. She held it to Laredo's lips. He drank greedily, water dribbling down his stubbled chin. When he was finished, she handed the canteen back to the deputy and then turned to Laredo.

'Are you able to talk, Mr. Judson?'

He nodded.

'Good. Then I'll get right to the point.'

'Wh-who are you?' he rasped.

'Someone who can keep you alive,' she replied. 'Now, kindly save your questions until I'm finished.'

Grudgingly, he fell silent.

'I'm here to make you an offer, Mr. Judson.'

'Call me Laredo.'

'If you accept, Mr. Judson, your death sentence will be commuted.'

'And if I don't?'

'You'll be marched right back to the gallows — and this time, I assure you, the rope will be fastened securely and you will most certainly die.'

'Some goddamn choice,' he growled.

'There'll be none of that!'

'None of what?'

'Taking the Lord's name in vain.'

Laredo almost laughed. He wanted to remind her that she was in a state penitentiary, not a Sunday school. But, not wanting to alienate her, he controlled himself and said: 'So why'd you put me through all this if you knew you were going to make me an offer?'

Ignoring his question, the woman said in the same articulate, no-nonsense voice: 'If you agree to my terms, you'll be released and given your guns and your horse. With them you're to track down and kill an outlaw by the name of Carson Nix. You've no doubt heard of him?'

'Sure. He's a vicious, sadistic sonofabitch who runs with the Cobb brothers down around Brownsville and Matamoros, Mexico — '

' — who so far has eluded all attempts to capture or kill him, and in the process has gunned down three lawmen and several posse members that pursued him,' she concluded.

'Reckon they knew the risk.'

'Small compensation for their wives and families.'

'Welcome to hard times.'

'That's a callous outlook.'

Laredo shrugged, unfazed. 'If I do kill Nix, what happens to me then?'

'You return here, to prison, and remain locked up until I find another target for you.'

'In other words, I'm your personal

assassin that you only turn loose whenever some renegade you can't catch needs to be killed?'

'Correct. Interested?'

'Maybe.'

'I need a more conclusive answer than that.'

Laredo said guardedly: 'If I do agree, how many lawmen ride with me?'

'None.'

'None?'

'If you need help, Mr. Judson, you're not the man for the job.'

'You must've figured I was, lady, or you wouldn't have saved my neck.'

'Never mind my reasons. What's your answer?' When he hesitated, she added: 'Forget it.'

'Forget what?'

'What you're considering.'

'Which is?'

'Making a break for Mexico once you've killed Nix.'

'What makes you think I'm thinking that?'

'Because it's what anyone in your

position would think.'

'Unless they had integrity.'

'Don't make me laugh.'

'Cynical as it seems, lady, there are still men who believe in honoring their word.'

'Not in your line of work. Besides,' she added caustically, 'you probably think you have nothing to lose by crossing the border.'

'You say that like you know different?'

The woman sighed, weary of his stalling, and said: 'What I know, Mr. Judson, is this: If you don't return here after killing Nix, I will take your son Ethan out of the home for mentally-retarded children he's presently in, change his name and lock him in a mental institution where you'll never find him.'

'Damn you! You'd do that?'

'In an instant.'

'To a young'un who's done you no harm?'

'It's an ugly thought, I agree. But yes,

in order to assure your return, I will do that.'

'Judas. Talk about integrity.'

'Integrity is a luxury neither of us can afford.'

'Now who's being callous?'

'The difference is, Mr. Judson, I don't pretend to be anything but what I am.'

'Which is?'

'A cold-hearted bitch who gets her job done at any cost.'

'And here I thought you were Joan of Arc.'

She smiled coldly. 'Nice to see your time in the prison library wasn't wasted.'

'It was better than breaking rocks.'

'Most things are. Now, I'd like your answer.'

'First, I need to know something.'

'What?'

'You've warned me what you'll do to Ethan if I *don't* return; now tell me what you'll do for him if I *do*.'

'You have my word that he'll be

placed in one of Charles Loring Brace's Children's Aid Society homes, where he'll be cared for as long as he lives. And since your boy is unable to cope in this world, you should find comfort in the fact that, no matter what happens to you, Ethan will never go without.'

'Sounds fair.'

'So, are you interested in my offer or not?'

'I'm interested,' Laredo said. 'But what about the Governor? The sonofabitch is hell bent on hanging me.'

'I'll handle the Governor.'

'You got that kind of clout?'

'The man I represent does. Now, for the last time, do you accept?'

'On one condition.'

'No conditions.'

'Then I reckon you better go fasten that rope.'

Sensing he was serious, the woman said: 'What's the condition?'

'After each killing, I get to spend time with my son.'

'That can be arranged. But you must return to the prison first.'

'Agreed.'

'And each visit will last only one hour and will be supervised by armed deputies.'

'Just in case I get any ideas 'bout trying to escape with Ethan?'

'Exactly.'

'How about two hours?'

'No. One hour or nothing.'

'Okay. Deal.'

'Excellent.' The woman turned to one of the prison guards. 'Take Mr. Judson back to his cell.'

'Wait,' Laredo said as the guards closed in. 'What's your name, lady?'

'My name is of no consequence to you.'

'It is if you want me to kill Nix.'

She looked surprised. 'You'd actually jeopardize your life and Ethan's future on something as inconsequential as my name?'

'Try me.'

'But why?'

14

'I like to know who's pulling my strings.'

'Very well . . . It's Miss Hargrove.'

'First name?'

'Miriam,' she said grudgingly.

'Mi-ri-am.' He repeated the name twice, each time enjoying the scowl that it brought to her face. 'Fits. I like it.'

'Now I'll die a happy woman.'

'I doubt that.'

'What's that supposed to mean?'

Laredo shrugged. 'My gut instinct tells me you ain't got the slightest idea of what happiness is.'

The truth stung.

The woman flushed angrily, rose and turned to the guards. 'Dammit. What are you waiting for? Take this prisoner back to his cell!'

3

It was almost dusk by the time Laredo finally reached Brownsville. The long, hot ride had exhausted both him and his horse Cisco. Reining in the sweat-soaked grullo, whose tan-gray coat and black mane and tail were caked with dust, he rode along Main Street.

It had only been six months since his last visit to the bawdy little cow-town, but in those months Brownsville had doubled in size. From what Laredo had heard from other convicts, lawlessness had also doubled, and he was watchful of each rider and pedestrian he passed. Over the years he'd acquired many enemies on both sides of the border, and didn't want weariness to dull his senses and possibly get him killed.

Brownsville, he knew, wasn't as civilized as its citizens wanted outsiders to believe. Founded beside the Rio Grande by Charles Stillman in 1849, the hot, dusty little town shared the U.S.-Mexican border with Matamoros, and presently was struggling to accommodate its fast-growing population. Every day more white settlers arrived with hopes and dreams, and though vastly outnumbered by Mexicans, they were determined to turn the sun-scorched but fertile land into farms or cattle ranches, and to open stores and businesses downtown.

Theirs was no easy task. Law and order was badly needed, since outlaws and border riffraff flourished in the cantinas and saloons that occupied almost every corner. But finding a lawman capable of taming the countless renegades had proven to be difficult; especially after the first two men who'd been sworn in as sheriff were gunned down almost as soon as they'd pinned on their stars. As a result, there'd been no more volunteers, leaving the streets of Brownsville unsafe for the townspeople. In an effort to remedy that, the locals were circulating a signed petition demanding that Governor Reed bring El Paso's celebrated Marshal Ezra Macahan to Brownsville, with orders to get rid of the lawless gunmen and drunken cowboys who were constantly shooting up the town.

Five such cowboys now galloped past Laredo, whooping it up and firing wildly into the air. He stubbornly held his line and at the last moment the cowboys split apart, cursing him as they rode past on either side of him. Laredo let them go without any rancor. Hell, it seemed like only yesteryear that he himself was hurrahing the streets of El Paso and the other burgeoning cattle towns that were spreading across Texas and New Mexico.

Besides, he had more important things on his mind. Carson Nix and the Cobb brothers frequented both Brownsville and Matamoros, its sister city across the border, and Laredo wanted to make sure he saw the outlaws before they saw him and wondered what the hell he was doing out of prison.

Miriam Hargrove had made it clear while accompanying him back to his cell that his mission was known only to them. And though he wasn't sure if he could trust her, he sensed that he could, and decided to continue thinking that way until she proved him wrong. Because of this, he knew that neither Nix nor the Cobb brothers would know why he'd been released from prison or why he was in Brownsville; however, that wasn't his only problem. Once, in Waco, he'd faced down the oldest Cobb, Lyman, in the Long Branch Saloon, calling him a gutless yellow back-shooter in front of everyone. He and the onlookers had expected Lyman to jerk his iron. But instead he refused to draw and slunk out of the saloon. A year had passed since then — a year in which neither Lyman nor his three brothers had sought any retribution.

Most Texans believed that the Cobbs had put the incident behind them. But not Laredo. He and the brothers had been feuding for years, and he knew they were merely biding their time, waiting for the right moment when they could avenge themselves by bushwhacking him.

Halfway into town Laredo glanced ahead and saw two white-aproned, mustachioed bartenders throwing a drunken cowboy out of the Empire Saloon. The young man tried to fight back, but he was no match for the barkeeps, and landed face-down in the muddy street.

Laredo, seeing he wasn't seriously hurt, turned his attention to the Empire. It was Carson Nix's favorite hangout and Laredo, wondering if the outlaw was in there now, guided his horse across the street to Hayley's Feed and Grain Store. Here, he dismounted and tied Cisco to the rail. He then loosened the cinch-strap, giving the grullo a breather, grabbed his rifle from the saddle boot, dodged an incoming Wells Fargo stagecoach and crossed to the saloon.

By now the drunken cowboy had lurched to his feet, drawn his Colt .45, and was staggering back to the saloon. Though loath to interfere in another man's business, Laredo felt unusual empathy for the slim, boyishly-handsome cowboy. He reminded Laredo of himself at that age. Knowing the youth was about to stir up the kind of trouble that would either get him killed or imprisoned, Laredo decided to stop him. Stepping close, he jammed his rifle against the cowboy's back.

'Hold it, young fella.'

Startled, the youth whirled around, almost losing his balance. Recovering, he stood there, drunkenly swaying, blearily trying to focus on Laredo. 'W-Wha' you want?'

'The gun,' Laredo said. 'Leather it.'

'Wha'?'

'I said, holster your iron.'

'Why should I?'

''Cause Mr. Winchester says so.'

The young cowboy looked at the rifle Laredo was aiming at him. But instead of being intimidated, he became more truculent. Swaying unsteadily, he drew himself up until he was almost as tall as Laredo, and said: 'Well, you can . . . can tell Mr. Winnesheter to go t'hell! An' the s-same goes for you, mister.'

Laredo wasted no more time. He brought his rifle down hard across the youth's wrist. Yelping, he dropped his Colt and took a wild, off-balance swing at Laredo.

Ducking it, Laredo jabbed the barrel of the rifle into the young cowboy's belly. The youth, who couldn't have been more than seventeen, doubled over, gasping for air, and sank to his knees.

Laredo picked up the Colt, dumped out the shells and tucked it in his belt. Then, grasping the youth by the shirt collar, he dragged him to a nearby water trough. Still sucking wind, the young cowboy offered no resistance as

Laredo jerked him upright and threw him into the trough. He hit the water with a splash and sank beneath the surface. Moments later he sat up, spluttering, gasping for breath, arms windmilling as he tried to punch an assailant he couldn't see.

Laredo put his boot against the young cowboy's chest and pushed him under. The youth struggled but couldn't escape. Laredo held him there until he was close to drowning, then let him up and dropped the Colt in the water beside him.

'D-Damn you, mister!' the young cowboy raged. 'I'll k-kill you for this!'

'You need to sober up first,' Laredo said. 'By then, I'll be hard to find.' He pushed the youth under the water again and headed for the Empire.

4

Mariachi music came from inside the big, false-fronted saloon. Laredo mounted the boardwalk and peered over the batwing doors. As usual, the saloon was packed to the walls with unruly border trash and drunken lawbreakers. Laredo quickly checked out the whores and seedy gunmen drinking at the bar and then did the same to the sober, cold-eyed gamblers playing poker at the tables occupying the rear of the smoke-filled room.

Nix and the Cobb brothers were not in either group, and Laredo sighed with relief. He knew he was just postponing the inevitable, but at least now he could rent a room for the night without fear of being shot while he was sleeping.

Going next door, he entered the two-story wood-frame boarding house and punched the bell on the front desk.

Shortly, a toad-shaped, stoop-shouldered woman with iron-gray hair pulled back from her homely wrinkled face emerged from the parlor. Known as Cross-Eyed Emma, she tilted her head sideways in order to see him with her dominant left eye.

'It's me, Miss Em,' he said, identifying himself. 'Laredo.'

'By the God that cursed me,' she exclaimed, revealing tobacco-stained teeth. 'I was a-wondering just yesterday what had become of you.'

'In a hog's ear you were!'

'No, no, it's true, *hombre*. Believe me.'

'I'd be happy to, Miss Em, if I didn't know that nothing happens in the whole of Texas that sooner or later don't reach your ears.'

She gave a croaking laugh befitting her toad-like appearance. 'Ever the charmer, eh, Laredo?'

'If I am, you're the only one who thinks so.'

Again, she gave a croaking laugh.

Then, taking a plug of chaw from her coarse brown dress, she bit off a chunk, tongued it into her cheek and offered the plug to Laredo. When he shook his head, she returned it to her pocket, saying: 'Be with us a spell, will you?'

'Depends.'

'If it's the law you're sweating, don't. It's marginal at best.'

'How 'bout enemies?'

'The list's too long to remember.'

'Then I'll narrow it down for you. Specifically, Carson Nix and the Cobb brothers.'

Cross-Eyed Emma snorted with disgust and spat tobacco juice into a can at her feet. 'That gutless, murdering trash? Hell, I ain't seen them since God last pissed vinegar.'

'You sure 'bout that?'

'That's a hell of a question coming from you.'

'Sorry, Miss Em. I ain't questioning your integrity. It's just I get a tad snarky when I'm a walking target.'

'Then you better find another line of work.'

'I would, 'cept I don't have the brains for much else.'

'Hogwalla! The real reason is 'cause you like wearing a star.'

'That too,' Laredo admitted. 'I also like helping folks. Like seeing 'em smile . . . or having 'em come up and shake my hand afterwards, thanking me for what I done.'

'So become a Bible thumper. Folks may hate the way you preach your sermons but they won't never shoot you for it.'

The idea was so ludicrous Laredo didn't bother to respond, saying instead: ''Sides, most of the time the work ain't that dangerous. Usually the troublemakers I deal with are town drunks or petty thieves or cowhands letting off steam after they've driven a herd of beef to the railheads in Wichita and Abilene.'

'Carson Nix ain't no drover,' Cross-Eyed Emma reminded.

'That's just the point. Nix, he's a different animal. He's evil to the bone. He not only gets pleasure out of killing . . . but makes the victim's death last longer by shooting 'em in the belly.'

She shrugged fatly. 'Could always give up the chase. Say you lost his trail once he crossed the Rio Bravo.' When Laredo looked offended, she added: 'It ain't exactly a lie anyways. You don't know where Nix is or you wouldn't be here, asking me if I seen him.'

'Which I'm already beginning to regret.'

'Then I'll put your mind at ease,' Cross-Eyed Emma said. 'It's been exactly ten days since I last saw the Cobb brothers.'

'And Nix?'

'Longer. 'Bout three or four weeks.'

'Did he come in here?'

'Uh-uh. I saw him staggering out of the Empire.'

'Were the Cobbs with him?'

'No. He was alone. Looked like he'd had a few too many. Had trouble getting on his horse. But once he did, he put the spurs to it and rode off.'

'Which direction — did you notice?'

'All directions,' she said, rolling her crossed eyes and cackling.

'Very funny,' Laredo said.

'Dammit, you're right, you *are* snarky!' Cross-Eyed Emma chidingly shook her head. 'Best I can tell you is, rumor has it he's soft on a woman on the outskirts of town. Don't know her name or where she lives, but if it ain't bat shit flying in the wind, could be Nix is there with her now.'

Laredo chewed on her answer, trying to decide if it represented good or bad news, and then said: 'Know of any other women he's soft on?'

Cross-Eyed Emma started to shake her head; then, as it hit her, said: 'I don't know how reliable this is, you understand, but there was a time not so long ago that Nix had a hankering for a young whore at Kate's Place. I don't know which one, though probably Kate does, but 'cording to some, Nix couldn't keep it in his pants whenever he was around her.'

'You think there's any truth in the rumor?'

'Hell, what kind of question is that?'

'You're right,' Laredo said. 'Forget I asked.'

'Any other questions?'

'Just one.'

'Shoot.'

'How 'bout the stairs — front and back — they still creaking?'

'Loud enough to wake the dead.'

'Reckon I'll be here a few days then.'

'Which room this time?'

'Don't matter. Just so long as it ain't the same room I slept in last time I was here.'

'Don't worry, *hombre*. Ida and a whiskey salesman from Kentuck' have already put their shoes under that bed. But even if they hadn't, I wouldn't have given you that room.'

'You ain't forgotten what I told you, then?'

' 'Being predictable',' Cross-Eyed Emma

quoted, ''will kill you quicker than a slow draw'.'

'Amen,' Laredo said, adding: 'When a fella knows your habits, Miss Em, he's already one step ahead of you. And in my world that can prove fatal.'

'That's using 'em.'

'What?'

'Brains. We all got 'em, but most folks treat 'em like strangers.'

'Most folks ain't living as close to the edge as me.'

'They'd a-been dead long ago if they was.' She took a key from a pigeonhole behind her and handed it to Laredo. 'While we're rolling the dice, *hombre*, anyone in particular you trying to avoid?'

'Rangers.'

Cross-Eyed Emma snorted. 'Don't sweat those Texas weasels. They know better than to buck me. Last time one of 'em flashed a badge at me I blasted it with ol' Doc here.' She indicated the shotgun under the counter. 'Took the fella's hand off along with it.'

'I remember the trial well,' Laredo said. 'Lasted all of twenty minutes.'

'Wouldn't've lasted that long if Judge Foley had been sober. Drunken old sot, first he gets the hiccups and then, after I cured him by making him hold his breath while sipping whiskey backwards from a glass, he thanks me by warning my lawyer not to testify for me. 'Leading the witness', he called it.'

Laredo, mimicking a lawyer's voice, said: ''Your Honor, my client has a God-given affliction and therefore cannot be blamed for this unfortunate accident, on 'count of she can't tell which direction she's looking or who she's looking at. Can you, Madam?''

Cross-Eyed Emma chortled and clapped her wrinkled, veined hands. 'You got one helluva memory there, *hombre.*'

'When needs be.'

She squinted at him with one off-center eye as if trying to decide if she should reveal something. Then, lowering her voice, she confided: 'I'll let you into a secret about that there trial — a secret which I ain't never told no one afore. Judge Foley, married rat bastard that he is, was secretly forking one of my gals. He knew I knew 'bout it and to buy my silence he ruled that the state had to find a doctor who could learn me how to point my good eye at the person I'm talking to.'

'How'd that work?'

'Like a tit dipped in honey.'

Laredo chuckled. 'Tell me more.'

'Less'n a week later this eye-doctor from Dallas showed up with spectacles, charts and a bunch of ten-dollar words that give me a headache just trying to pronounce 'em. But I got to admit, when he was all done showing me what to do, I could see folks a heap better.'

'Nice to know the law's good for something,' Laredo said with a hint of bitterness. Then, handing her some money with 'This should cover it,' he started upstairs to his room.

5

It was full-on dark when Laredo next awoke. Taking out his timepiece, he held it close to his eyes so he could make out the position of the hands, and saw it was almost nine o'clock. Rising, he leaned over the basin atop the battered chest of drawers, splashed cold water on his face and toweled himself dry. He then combed his shaggy black hair back with his fingers and donned his gray, flat-crowned hat, buckled on his gun-belt and drew his Peacemaker. Like most gunmen and desert riders, he kept only five shells in his Colt. That way, if he accidentally dropped his gun, the hammer would fall on an empty chamber and he wouldn't shoot himself in the foot. But today he decided he might need that extra round, so he removed a cartridge from his belt and slipped it into the cylinder. Then, holstering the Colt, he put on his denim jacket and cautiously opened the door. The narrow hallway was dark and reeked of stale beer. Making sure he was alone, Laredo locked his door and moved quietly toward the back stairs.

Outside, drifting clouds darkened the moon. A warm dry wind came gusting up from the border. It made his eyes prickle, reminding him they were drying out. He dug into his jeans for his eye-drops, then remembered that he'd forgotten to refill the prescription.

Angry with himself, he continued on down the rickety, creaking stairway. He'd had trouble with his eyes for several years now, and the bespectacled little German eye-doctor he'd grudgingly visited in Austin had explained that his tear ducts had quit working, and prescribed eye-drops. He'd also warned Laredo that his near-sightedness was worsening, and suggested he should consider wearing glasses. To prove his point, the doctor had had Laredo try on the latest eyewear, a pair of octagon-shaped wire-framed spectacles that could be worn on or off a horse.

Laredo couldn't deny he saw better with the spectacles. But, as he explained to the doctor, an ex-lawman-turned-bounty-hunter wearing glasses was an open invitation for every outlaw and gunman to use him for target practice. Besides, he added, he'd recently discovered that if he squinted he could still see pretty well.

By now he'd reached the bottom of the stairs. Pausing in the dark alley Laredo rubbed his eyes, blinking until tears came. It was another trick he'd learned. It wasn't as effective as eye-drops, but it lubricated his eyes for at least two hours. Able to see now, he squinted in both directions. He wasn't expecting trouble, but that didn't mean it wasn't lurking there. Besides, he knew it was these ingrained precautionary habits that had kept him alive these past thirty-odd years.

Satisfied the alley was empty, he

hurried to the rear of the Empire Saloon. The door to the kitchen was unlocked and he opened it quietly. The Mexican help stopped working as he entered. They all knew him and greeted him with smiles. He pressed his finger to his lips. They nodded to show they understood, and watched with dark, curious eyes as he moved, between the big iron stove and the pots and pans hanging by the sink, to the door leading into the saloon.

Opening the door a little, he squinted until he could make out the faces of the men drinking at the bar. He recognized some of them from 'Wanted' posters he'd seen pinned on walls and fences during his ride here from Huntsville. But none of them ran with Nix or the Cobb brothers, so Laredo shifted his gaze to the poker players. Same result. Disappointed, he was about to enter the bar for a drink, when three familiar figures pushed in through the batwing doors.

Laredo stepped back and peered

through the crack in the door. Squinting, he watched as, after a few steps, the Cobb brothers paused and warily looked around. Then, satisfied there were no lawmen present, they elbowed their way through the crowd to the bar. The gunmen standing there, hard cases themselves, bristled and angrily reached for their guns. But when they saw who was crowding them, they quickly changed their minds and made room for the Cobbs.

Wondering where Carson Nix was, Laredo continued to watch the three brothers. Usually, Nix and the Cobbs were inseparable. And the fact that tonight they weren't together made him uneasy. He glanced over his shoulder to make sure that Nix wasn't sneaking up behind him. Satisfied he wasn't, Laredo faced front, widening his gaze so that he could watch the entrance and the Cobbs at the same time.

Ten minutes passed. By then several known gunmen had entered the saloon, but none of them was Nix. Frustrated,

Laredo decided to wait another five minutes, promising himself that if Nix didn't show by then, he'd start looking for the outlaw in the other saloons and cantinas.

Waiting wasn't easy for Laredo. He prided himself on being a man of action, who always faced trouble head-on, and it galled him now not to confront the Cobbs and force them to tell him where Nix was. But he knew that once they saw him, they would try to kill him. And then, even if he survived the shootout, he'd lose the advantage of surprising Carson Nix — which was his best chance of killing the outlaw — and be forced to return to prison without accomplishing his mission, something he had no intention of doing. Because, although Miriam Hargrove had never mentioned it, Laredo sensed that if he failed to kill Nix, she wouldn't offer him another target. Worse, she wouldn't take care of Ethan. And since his son was mentally deficient, as she'd pointed out, the boy would always find life a painful uphill struggle!

A loud, boisterous laugh interrupted Laredo's thinking. It came from a huge bearded man standing beside the oldest Cobb brother, Lyman. Wearing an old bearskin coat, a string of bear claws around his neck and a soiled campaign hat, the man towered over everyone. Laredo recognized him from previous times he'd been in Brownsville, and also from 'Wanted' posters that offered a five-hundred-dollar reward for the capture of Big Bill 'Claws' Blackburn. A train and bank robber, he was also a braggart and a bully, who enjoyed picking fights with smaller men that he killed by bear-hugging them until he broke their backs.

Even as Laredo watched, Claws laughed again at something the barkeep said, this time stepping back and bumping into Lyman. Beer spilled over the gunfighter. Cursing Claws, Lyman went for his six-gun. Fast as he was, his Colt hadn't cleared leather when Claws back-handed him, slamming Lyman against the bar.

Claws was on him instantly. They grappled for a moment, Claws trying to bear-hug him. But Lyman was too quick and broke free. Cursing, Claws whipped out a long-bladed pig-sticker and went to stab Lyman. He would have succeeded but for the other Cobb brothers, Heck and Travis. They shot him several times in the chest and belly, the roar of their six-shooters drowning out all other sounds in the crowded saloon.

Claws staggered back against the bar, hands clasped over his wounds, belching blood.

Leering, Lyman beckoned the dying man forward. 'C'mon, you chucklehead,' he taunted. 'Come on, come on, don't stop now. Give me a hug.' With a mocking grin, he watched as Claws took one lurching step forward and halted.

'What's the matter, big man?' Lyman jeered. 'Someone hogtie you?'

Claws stood there, swaying, his expression a mixture of pain and confusion.

Lyman laughed, pressed his gun against Claws' brow and pulled the trigger.

The slug punched a neat round hole in the big man's forehead. His head snapped back, blood spurting over his bearded face. For one long moment he stood there, swaying, eyes glazed, then he crumpled and was dead before he hit the floor.

The Cobb brothers immediately formed a back-to-back circle, guns cocked, heads swiveling to see if any of Claws' friends were going to seek revenge.

None did. Instead, they all callously turned back to the bar as if nothing unusual had happened, and continued talking.

Laredo watched and waited. Everyone ignored the corpse, newcomers and the men at the bar alike stepping over it as if it were a piece of litter or a drunk sleeping it off.

Satisfied they weren't going to be

attacked, the Cobb brothers holstered their guns, returned to the bar and finished their drinks. Then, while Claws' blood was still reddening the trampled sawdust, they turned and swaggered out of the saloon.

Laredo, not wanting to lose them, left the kitchen and elbowed his way through the jostling crowd to the entrance. There, he looked over the batwing doors in time to see the brothers crossing the street to their horses — three leggy, deep-chested bays bred to run all day, tied up outside an old saloon nicknamed Coffin Varnish.

Laredo waited for the Cobbs to mount and ride away before hurrying to his horse. The weary grullo had been dozing and wasn't pleased to see him. It nipped at him, missed, and tried to cow-kick him. Laredo, aware of the horse's ill-temper, avoided the kick and warned Cisco to calm down. Then he tightened the girth strap, stepped up into the saddle and rode after the brothers.

6

He hadn't far to ride. At the next corner the Cobbs dismounted and tied up their horses outside Whalen's Livery Stable. Laredo reined up in the shadows close behind them but remained in the saddle, hoping they would lead him to Nix.

Briefly the brothers horsed around, playfully punching each other and arguing about something. Laredo couldn't hear what they were saying, but by their gesturing, guessed it involved money. Finally coming to an agreement, they crossed the street and entered a plain-looking two-story wooden building that housed a brothel known by everyone as Kate's Place.

Laredo, frustrated by his inability to find Nix, cursed his bad luck. He didn't want to follow the Cobbs into the whorehouse. Not because he was a prude or was against paying for sex, but because he and the owner, Collette Babineaux, were old friends, and he didn't want to involve her in any kind of gunfight.

Collette was a petite, refined widow with mannishly short black hair and powdered skin, who, years ago, had been Brownsville's first madam. Though she came from New Orleans and was of French heritage, for reasons no one could remember she was called Kansas City Kate — or just Kate. Shunned at first, over the years she'd finally earned the respect of everyone — even the shrewish, sour-faced Ladies of the Christian Temperance Union — for having polite girls, clean beds and fair prices.

She and Laredo had bonded during his first visit. Then in his early twenties, he had been embarrassingly shy. Noticing this, she'd taken him under her wing. From then on she had treated him more like a son than a steady customer, often inviting him to dinner in her elegant quarters above the carriage house.

Laredo, born to migrant dirt-farmers, had never seen such finery. The flowered silk drapes were imported from China, the Oriental rugs from Persia, the furniture from England — the delicate Queen Anne chairs so fragile that at first he'd been afraid to sit on them. Fragrant incense burned day and night, hiding the smell of the Mexican cigarillos that Kate chain-smoked. Though kind and patient with him, she was obsessed with cleanliness and insisted he always wash his hands in rose-scented water before eating.

Laredo didn't mind washing, but disliked how he smelled afterward. But he never complained for fear of offending Kate. Neither did he complain about the French cuisine that had names he couldn't pronounce — though he longed for a burned steak, fried potatoes and a beer. He also felt awkward eating off snowy linen table-cloths and using polished silverware, flanked by ornate gold candlesticks, but again he said nothing. He even learned to ignore the disdainful looks Kate's long-time maid — a haughty, turban-headed mulatto named Rosette Laveau — gave him as she served them. Inside, though, it riled him. After all, she was a former slave who should have known her place —

Gunshots jolted Laredo back to the present. Two drunks galloped past, hollering and firing into the air. As Laredo watched them, he realized why Carson Nix and the Cobbs weren't together. Nix was sweet on one of the young Creole whores, and Laredo guessed the outlaw had chosen to be with her while the brothers quenched their thirst at the Empire.

But now they were all together in Kate's Place, presenting Laredo with a dilemma. He knew he couldn't flush Nix out without endangering Kate or her girls, something he was loath to do. At the same time, he knew if he didn't kill Nix now, the outlaw might elude him forever. And if that happened, Laredo guessed he'd either hang or spend the rest of his days in prison, preventing him from looking after the one person who needed him most: Ethan!

Thinking of his son made his choice easier. Laredo rode on around behind the whorehouse, dismounted and climbed the outside stairway to the second floor. Due to the lingering heat the bedroom windows were open, and Laredo could hear the whores giggling with their customers. He paused at the rear door and listened, trying to distinguish the men's voices. He heard the Cobb brothers talking coarsely to the girls they'd chosen, but couldn't hear Nix.

Drawing his Peacemaker, he inched open the door. Ahead on the wall to his left, an oil lamp cast eerie shadows in the dimly lit hallway. Everything looked blurry to him. He blinked and rubbed his dry eyes, bringing tears to them. As his failing vision cleared, he saw that the doors to the four bedrooms were closed. Cracks of light showed under them.

He crept to the first bedroom and put his ear against the door. The man talking inside was Lyman. Laredo moved to the door opposite and listened. The voices belonged to Heck and Travis. Laredo sighed, wondering if he'd made a mistake about Nix being there at all. He started for the third bedroom when suddenly the door nearest the stairs opened and a shadowy figure stepped out. The same size and build as Nix, the man paused and buckled on his gun-belt.

Laredo froze, Colt in hand.

The man didn't see Laredo, but sensed someone was there. Whirling around, he went for his gun.

Laredo, knowing how fast Nix could slap leather, fired.

The boom of his Colt echoed deafeningly in the narrow dim hallway.

The man staggered, grasped the bannisters to support himself, lost his grip and fell head-first down the narrow stairs.

Moments later the other doors burst open and the Cobbs charged out, guns drawn.

Judson fanned his Colt and gunned down the brothers.

Screams came from the whores in the bedrooms. Two of them fearfully peered out, their screams increasing as they saw the three bloody corpses.

Laredo yelled at them to get back in their rooms. As they obeyed, he made sure the Cobb brothers were dead, and then hurried downstairs to make sure Nix was dead too.

Kate had gotten there first and was kneeled beside the body. She looked up as Laredo approached, met his gaze and shrugged to let him know that she didn't know if the man would live or die.

Laredo leathered his Colt and knelt beside her. That was when he saw the victim's face and felt a stab in his heart.

The man lying on the floor, bleeding from a bullet wound along his temple, was the young handsome cowboy that earlier Laredo had tried to sober up by pushing him into the water trough.

Laredo stared at the youth in stunned disbelief. He knew God could be cruel, but surely not even God was cruel enough to put him through the same ordeal twice . . .

He needn't have worried. Even as he railed against God's injustice, the young cowboy's eyelids fluttered.

Kate grabbed Laredo's arm. 'L-Look! Look, he's alive!'

Laredo sagged with relief.

Kate looked up at one of the naked whores watching from over the bannisters, and yelled: 'Hattie! Go fetch Doc Sheldon! Now!' she added when the whore didn't move. 'Dammit, girl, hurry! Hurry! Go, go, go . . . '

The naked whore galloped down the stairs and started for the front door.

'Wait! Here — cover yourself!' Kate threw her shawl over the naked girl, who pulled it about her and ran out the door.

7

Miriam Hargrove and her three special deputies stepped off the early morning train from San Antonio and were greeted by Mayor Deke Fulton. Flanking him on the narrow platform were two elderly members of the Town Council. Despite it being unusually cool, the three men were nervously sweating and looked as if they hadn't slept in days.

'Thank heavens you're finally here,' the Mayor exclaimed. 'Another day of this madness, and, well — I swear I don't know what we would've done.'

Miriam ignored his welcoming outstretched hand and said irritably: 'For God's sake, Mayor, pull yourself together! You're making this sound like a national crisis.'

'Well, I don't know what you would call a national crisis, Miss Hargrove,' he

53

replied peevishly, 'but we've got three men digging buckshot out of their posteriors and — '

She cut him off. 'Mayor Fulton, kindly spare me the gory details! Who got shot or where is of no concern to me. I'm neither a sheriff nor a Federal Marshal.'

'I'm well aware of that, Miss Hargrove.'

'Then why the devil didn't you wire the marshal's office in El Paso or the Rangers' headquarters in Austin, and ask *them* for help?'

'I wanted to, believe me. But he — Laredo — asked specifically for you. Said if we brought in Rangers, or any other lawmen he'd come out and shoot us all!'

'And you believed him?'

'Why not? He's full of whisky and pissed at the world!'

'He's also got a scattergun and enough shells to fight a goddamn war,' added one of the Councilmen.

'Yeah,' agreed the other. 'And the

belligerent sonofabitch is just itching to shoot us!'

'Nonsense!' Miriam said. 'In case your feeble minds have forgotten, Laredo Judson was once a highly respected lawman. No matter how low he's sunk or how drunk he is, he would never deliberately kill an unarmed man. Any man. Not even a — politician.'

'Perhaps you'd be kind enough to go in there and tell *him* that,' said the Mayor. 'Because apparently it's slipped his memory.'

'He's just bluffing, for God's sake! Can't you see that? He — ' She broke off, then quickly added: 'In where? Where's he holed up?'

'The Empire.'

The tallest of the special deputies stepped close to Miriam and whispered in her ear.

She shook her head. 'No, Jason. I appreciate your offer but I'll go in alone. I don't know why Judson asked for me. We've only met once and that was hardly a social visit. But if he wants to talk to me, I'll gladly oblige him. No point in exacerbating the problem.' To the Mayor, she added: 'This saloon — the Empire — is it within walking distance?'

'Yes, but we brought a buckboard and a wagon.'

'What on earth for? Did you expect me to bring a posse to subdue one man?'

Rebuked, the Mayor reddened. 'This isn't just any one man, Miss Hargrove. This is Laredo Judson, a man who's killed more men than John Wesley Hardin!'

'Difference is,' Miriam replied, 'all the men Judson killed were outlaws who deserved to die.'

'Maybe so,' the Mayor said. 'But right now, liquored-up like he is, I doubt if Laredo knows the difference 'tween good and bad. Or worse, even cares. He's just dead set on shooting anyone who comes near the saloon!'

'We'll see about that,' Miriam said. 'Meanwhile, have some of your men unload our horses and saddle them. I doubt if we'll need them, but it's best to be prepared.'

'Consider it done,' the Mayor said. He looked at the nearest Councilman, who nodded to show he'd take care of it. The Mayor then led Miriam and her deputies to an awaiting buckboard and wagon parked near the station-house.

Miriam kept silent until she'd climbed aboard the buckboard. Then she gave the Mayor a withering look and said: 'What about hostages?'

'What about them?'

'Is Judson holding any in the saloon?'

The Mayor shook his head. He disliked this woman intensely, but was too intimidated by her to stand his ground.

'So what you're saying is, Judson's in there by himself?'

'Uh . . . not exactly.'

'*Not exactly*? What the hell's that supposed to mean?'

'The bartender, Art Shepherd's, in there with him. But he isn't a hostage.'

'How do you know that?'

''Cause Laredo would never shoot him or stop him from leaving anytime he wanted.'

'Then why's he still in there?'

'He and Laredo are old pals,' the Mayor said lamely.

'*Old pals?*'

'Yeah. They grew up together.'

'How ducky.'

Ignoring her sarcasm, the Mayor said: 'I told Art to come out, but he refused. Said he was sticking with Laredo till this mess was resolved.'

'Loyalty . . . ' Miriam spat out the word as if it were distasteful. 'Was there ever an act so widely misconstrued?' To the Mayor, she added sarcastically: 'Any *more* surprises?'

'There's no one else in the saloon, if that's what you mean.'

'Except Lobo, of course,' reminded one of the Councilmen.

'Lobo?'

'Art's wolfdog. He goes everywhere with him. He's like Art's second shadow.'

Miriam rolled her dark, expressive eyes. 'Good God Almighty,' she breathed. 'All we need now is a dancing bear and we'd have ourselves a three-ring circus!'

8

In the Empire, Laredo hadn't slept or drawn a sober breath since shooting the young cowboy two days ago. Bad as he looked, he felt even worse. He stood at the long mahogany bar, leaning on his elbows, fighting to stay awake. In one fist he clutched a near-empty bottle of whisky, while the other hand rested on the stock of the Remington double-barreled shotgun lying before him.

Nearby, Art Shepherd sat on a stool, slumped over the bar, dozing on his folded arms. At his feet lay Lobo, a huge Mexican wolf-mastiff mix that two years ago Art had rescued from a fight ring in Matamoros, where the dog was pitted against a black bear. Game as Lobo was, the bear's size and strength were too overpowering, and by the time Art had persuaded the owner to sell Lobo, the bear's claws had slashed the dog's belly open, exposing his entrails. Everyone told Art he was a damned fool for wasting his money on a dying mongrel. But Art bought him anyway and, with a vet's help, nurtured Lobo back to health. From that day on, the two were inseparable; with Lobo's loyalty so intense that no one dared get too close to Art for fear of being attacked by the wolfdog.

At the bar Laredo yawned wearily and fought to keep his eyes open. But gradually they closed and he nodded off. As his chin bumped his chest, he awakened with a start and looked about him, bleary-eyed and belligerent. Then, reassured by the familiar surroundings, he relaxed and nudged Art, asking: 'Any of that cat-piss you call coffee left?'

'Sure.' Art got off his stool, went behind the bar and grabbed a pot of coffee resting on the back counter. 'Want me to heat it up?'

'Cold's fine.'

Art filled two mugs, handed one to Laredo and drank from the other.

'So-help-me-Jesus,' he said, grimacing. 'If that don't kill you, nothing will.'

Laredo didn't seem to notice as he gulped down the lukewarm black coffee. 'I ever tell you 'bout my boy?' he asked, staring wistfully into the mug.

'Many times,' Art said gently. 'Ethan, right?'

'Could've been him, you know — when he grows up, I mean.'

'Who?'

'Young fella I shot.'

'But it wasn't, hoss.'

'No, but it could've been,' Laredo insisted. 'And that's the ugly part of it.'

'So you made a mistake. Happens to everyone. Especially if your life's on the line. I mean, look at it this way: what if it *had* been Nix and you hadn't pulled the trigger? Then instead of sitting here drinking tangle-leg and coffee, you'd be six feet under.'

'And better off for it, too.'

'How you figure that?'

''Least then I wouldn't be killing innocent folks.'

'And your boy — would he be better off watching grave-diggers lower your corpse in the ground?'

Laredo didn't answer. Draining the whisky bottle, he hurled it across the room where it shattered against the far wall. Instantly Lobo raised his massive head, growled, and looked protectively at Art.

'It's okay, fella,' Art assured the wolfdog, which thumped its furry tail and went back to sleep. 'Now, what were you rattling on about?' he asked Laredo.

'Life.'

'What about it?'

'Piss on it,' Laredo said. 'It's a never-ending uphill struggle you can't win.'

'Welcome to hard times, as you're always saying.'

Laredo squinted at his blurred reflection in the big ornate mirror behind the bar. 'Know what, *amigo*?'

'Tell me.'

'Way I figure, now that my eyesight's

going, it ain't safe to be in the same goddamn town as me.'

'Never was,' Art said. 'Far back as I can remember, even when you could see fine, you were always a mean, wild-assed, cantankerous sonofabitch.'

'I was?'

'Damn' right. Only difference now, hoss, is you're an *old*, mean, wild-assed, cantankerous sonofabitch.'

'No disputing that,' Laredo admitted. He grabbed his empty mug and threw it at the mirror. It shattered and shards of broken glass flew everywhere.

This time Lobo jumped up, bared his fangs at Laredo and growled.

'Shut up,' Laredo told it. 'Or I'll throw you back in the pit with the bear.'

'There's nothing he'd like better,' Art said, grinning. 'Ain't that right, Lobo?' He coaxed the big dog into a back room, closed the door and rejoined Laredo. 'I hope you're enjoying yourself, hoss. 'Cause everything you break goes on your tab — 'long with about ten gallons of red-eye.'

If Laredo heard him, he didn't show it. He continued to stare, bleary-eyed, at the now-blank wall where the mirror frame still hung.

'Dammit, quit blaming yourself,' Art grumbled. 'You heard what Doc Sheldon said: there's a chance the young fella will come out of the coma.'

''Remote chance' is what he said.'

'Still a chance. And that's what you should be focusing on.'

'Oh, I'm focusing on it,' growled Laredo. 'I've been focusing on it and nothing else for three goddamn days and nights!'

'Okay, so it's taking longer than the Doc expected. That still don't mean it won't happen — ' Art broke off as he heard footsteps approach along the boardwalk.

Laredo heard them too. Grabbing the shotgun, he thumbed back both hammers and aimed the gun at the batwing doors.

'Whoever you are,' he warned, 'if you

want to see sunup, stay the hell out of here.'

The footsteps continued to draw near. 'Judson,' a voice called out, 'it's me, Miriam Hargrove. I'm coming in.'

Art quickly pressed the shotgun down. 'Don't shoot, hoss. It's her — the woman you told the Mayor to send for.'

'Come ahead,' Laredo yelled. 'But move slow and easy and keep your hands where I can see 'em. And make sure you're alone.'

'I'm quite alone,' Miriam replied, 'of that I can assure you.' Her face appeared above the batwing doors. 'Now quit being an ass, Judson, and put that gun down!'

'Do like she says, hoss,' Art pleaded.

Grudgingly, Laredo set the scatter-gun on the bar, but kept his hand on it.

Miriam pushed the doors open and approached without fear. 'As you can see,' she said, opening her coat, 'I'm unarmed.'

Laredo eyed her suspiciously. 'What do you want?'

'I don't want anything,' she said. 'You sent for me, remember?'

Unable to deny that, Laredo grumbled: 'I never figured you'd show.'

'Then why'd you send for me?'

Her bluntness stumped him.

'Well?' she demanded.

'I figured . . . thought maybe, just maybe, you'd be the one person who'd understand.'

'Understand what?' she said, joining him at the bar. 'That you've let two bad breaks change you from a trusted, respected lawman into a bitter, irresponsible drunk?'

'*Two bad breaks*?' Laredo erupted. 'You call killing a pair of innocent young men — not much more'n boys, really — 'two bad breaks'?'

'What else should I call them? And on top of that, the second boy hasn't died — yet!'

Laredo couldn't think of a suitable retort.

His silence irked Miriam. 'Men!' she said disgustedly. 'If you aren't a sorry bunch. You all act like you're hard as nails yet underneath, you're so damned soft and sentimental it makes me sick.'

Her words cut deep. Laredo glared at her. 'I was wrong about you, lady. Dead wrong. Your kind would never understand.'

'*My* kind?' Miriam snorted. 'How the hell do you know what my kind is? You barely know me.'

'Oh, I know you,' Laredo said bitterly. 'I've dealt with you on every jury I've faced. You all sit there looking so prim and proper, passing judgment on lawmen for doing the very thing you hired them to do.'

'So that's it,' Miriam said. 'You're blaming all women because a few female jurors didn't rush to your defense.'

Laredo's grim, tight-lipped silence verified her accusation.

Miriam sighed and lost her aggressiveness. 'Oh, Judson, for heaven's sake grow up! Everyone gets the short end of the stick now and then. You just have to deal with it.' Pausing, she turned to Art and indicated the coffee pot. 'May I have a cup of that, please?'

'Sure thing.' Art filled another mug and set it on the bar in front of her. 'I should warn you, though, ma'am, it's been sitting 'round for a spell. Could be a mite strong.'

'Just how I like it.'

'I don't have no cream or sugar neither.'

'Black's fine, thank you.' Raising the mug, she took a sip. Instantly, she grimaced, eyes saucers, and gave a rueful smile. 'Would it be rude of me to inquire how many people you've killed with this?'

'Reckon I've lost count,' Art grinned, feeling better now that Miriam was there.

'I don't doubt it,' she said. Then to Laredo: 'All right, Judson. I'm here. What do you want to talk to me about?'

'Prison.'

'What about it?'

'I want you to fix it so I can go back inside.'

His request caught her off-guard. She looked at Art, who shrugged as if it was beyond him, and then turned back to Laredo. 'You sure that's what you want?'

'Positive.'

'What about your son?'

'He'll be better off without me.'

'Oh, for . . . ' Miriam scowled, exasperated. 'You know, Judson, if there's anything I hate worse than a quitter, it's a whining quitter, which apparently you've become.'

'Think what you please,' he said. 'I still want to go back to prison.'

She studied him, trying to figure out what made him tick. Then she reached into her pocket — a move that made Laredo instantly grab for the shotgun.

'Easy,' she said, taking something out. 'It's just a photograph.'

Laredo watched warily as Miriam set the photo before him. He stared at it, lack of sleep and too much whisky making it hard for him to focus. Rubbing his eyes, he blinked, causing tears, then picked up the photograph and studied it.

'Who's this?'

'You don't recognize your own son?'

Shocked, Laredo stared at the small, vacant-eyed boy absently sucking his thumb in the photo. 'That's Ethan?'

Miriam nodded. 'Taken a few days ago.'

'I never would've known.'

'That's why I brought it,' she said. 'I knew you hadn't seen him in a month of Sundays and thought you might like to see how much he's grown up.'

Laredo held the photo closer to his eyes, curious to see how big his son had gotten.

'How's he doing?'

'All things considered, as well as can be expected.'

Laredo nodded, but couldn't help feeling dejected by the sight of his hapless son.

As if feeling his pain, Miriam said:

'His teachers say he's very bright considering his condition. Very polite, too.'

'I'm glad,' Laredo said flatly.

'He may not be the son you hoped for,' Miriam said, reading his sour expression, 'but he's still your flesh and blood, Judson, and doesn't deserve to be neglected just because of something that wasn't his fault.'

'You saying it was my fault — or my wife's?'

'Of course not. Unfortunately, these things just happen.'

'Yeah.'

'You say that as if tragedy only strikes you. It doesn't, believe me. Sadly, children such as yours are born every day.'

'So much for God's compassion.'

'That kind of response is beneath you.'

'Oh, so now you know all about me, huh?'

'No. Just enough to question your responsibility.'

'Lady, you couldn't be farther north of the truth. Thanks to them blood-sucking Comanches, responsibility roped me in almost 'fore I could walk!'

His remark sobered Miriam.

'What,' Laredo said, 'no sarcastic response?'

Stung, she said: 'That's uncalled-for, Judson.'

Laredo laughed mirthlessly and continued as if she hadn't spoken. 'Well, for what it's worth, lady, I may not be knee-deep in compassion — but responsibility? That's a horse of another color. I've never ducked responsibility in my life — and that includes my boy. Reckon you can ask anyone that.'

'I already did,' Miriam said. 'And you came through with flying colors.'

Laredo grunted in a way that could have meant anything.

'So,' Miriam said, 'do you still want to go back behind the walls?'

He didn't trust himself to reply.

'I was hoping this picture would

change your mind.'

'And if it did?'

Miriam shrugged. 'You tell me.'

Laredo looked deep inside himself and didn't like the person he saw.

'You'd be doing both me and the state a favor if you did agree,' Miriam continued. 'I mean, let's face it: you're the only man I know who's capable of bringing Nix in.'

Laredo chewed on her words, thinking they sounded suspiciously like flattery.

'If Carson Nix has slapped to Mexico, like I figure,' he said finally, 'it might take me a while to run him to ground.'

'So?'

'I don't want you to think I've ducked out on you if I'm not in touch for a spell.'

'There's no deadline. Just bring Nix back. That's all I ask.'

'Dead or alive?'

'Since when did that matter to you, Judson?'

Laredo grinned for the first time in two days. 'You're a real peach, Miss Hargrove.'

'So I've been told,' Miriam said. Rising, she added to Art, 'Work on that coffee, Mr. Shepherd.'

'Will do, ma'am.'

Miriam picked up the shotgun and went to the door. From there she said to Laredo: 'I assume I can tell the Mayor that you won't be shooting anyone else for a while?'

'You can count on it — *Miriam*.'

'I am — *Laredo*.' She pushed out through the batwing doors and walked off.

Laredo turned to Art. 'You know, after I lost Helen, I figured that was it for me.'

''Bout finding another wife, you mean?'

Laredo nodded.

'And now?'

Laredo looked wistfully toward the door. 'Could be I was a tad hasty, *amigo*.'

'Damn,' Art said.

'Damn, what?'

'You're a hard one to figure out.'

'Meaning?'

'Listening to you and that woman swapping barbs, I would've bet the farm that you hated each other.'

Laredo shrugged as if he too didn't understand. Then, 'You know what they say 'bout love and hate, *amigo*. They're both fueled by the same emotion.'

9

Dr. James Sheldon, a spry old bachelor who'd fought alcoholism for most of his adult life, lived at the edge of town, facing the river, in a small clapboard house that served as his office and living quarters. He greeted Laredo with a warm smile and invited him in for a cup of the 'best damn' coffee west of Missouri!'

Laredo gladly accepted. As he sipped the hot, fresh-brewed black coffee, he asked the doctor if the young cowboy had come out of his coma yet.

'Yes. 'Bout an hour ago,' Dr. Sheldon replied. 'That's why I sent for you.'

Laredo sagged with relief. 'Then he's going to live?'

'Oh, sure. For a long time, hopefully. Truth is, the young man could be on his way right now. But I figured another day of rest would serve him well.

Come,' he added, 'I'll introduce you to him.'

'No, thanks,' Laredo said. 'Reckon I done him enough harm already.'

'Nonsense. You — '

''Sides, it's time I was making dust. I still got supplies to buy, and every second I stay here gives Carson Nix another second to get farther away. But you could do me a favor,' Laredo said, handing the doctor an envelope. 'Give this to your patient. He could most likely use some traveling money.'

'That's a fact,' Dr. Sheldon said. 'Boy's got nothing but trail dust in his pockets.'

'Figures.'

'A malady, if I recall correctly, you've experienced from time to time?'

'Amen,' Laredo chuckled. Taking out some money, he added: 'I'd like to pay for whatever the youngster owes you.'

'Thanks but no thanks,' Dr. Sheldon said. 'I mean it,' he insisted, pushing Laredo's money away. 'Good Lord, if I started charging for every bullet of yours I dug out of some feisty young gunslinger, folks might mistake me for a real doctor.' Grinning, he offered his hand to Laredo and they shook warmly. 'Ride safely, my friend.'

'Always.' Laredo opened the door and went out to his horse.

Horst's Emporium was one of Brownsville's first enterprises. Originally a modest little general store, over the years it had grown into a large, bustling mercantile business whose slogan boasted: 'We have all your needs. If we don't have what you want, tell us and we'll get it for you!'

Laredo knew the owners — Heinrich and his blond, big-hipped, adoring wife Gerda — well. He liked them both, as did everyone else in town, and always took the time to visit with them whenever he was in Brownsville. Heinie responded by never failing to invite Laredo into his office, where the two friends swapped stories over a bottle of Schnapps taken from Heinie's private stock.

Nicknamed the 'Little Emperor,' Heinie was a small, amiable man of fifty who wore a monocle, had an upturned mustache with waxed tips and spoke with a thick German accent. A non-typical Prussian, he was eager to please, and quick to deflect the praise showered on him for the emporium's success onto his wife. But he fooled no one with his so-called modesty: on the contrary, they considered it an endearing trait that merely added to his popularity.

Laredo knew differently though. He was one of the few people who knew the truth about Heinie's part in the growth of the emporium. That was because once, a few years back when the storekeeper had had one too many Schnapps, he confided in Laredo that without Gerda's strength and driving ambition the business would never have succeeded.

Laredo laughed knowingly. 'I know better, *amigo*. You're just saying that 'cause you love your wife, you old Prussian!'

'Ya, ya, ya,' Heinie insisted. 'While it is most true zat I do love my dear sweet Gerda, it is equally true zat deep down I am zer most lazy man.'

'You?' Laredo said, amused. 'Hell, *amigo*, you're the least lazy fella I ever met.'

'Zis is vat I fool everyone into thinking, ya,' Heinie admitted. 'But thinking zis way does not mean it is true. Zer real reason I keep inside like a secret. I am not lazy because my beloved Gerda, she vill not permit me to be zo.'

'Gerda? What's she got to do with it?'

'Everything, *mein lieber Freund*. It is Gerda who make zer many goals for me, goals I must achieve, she say, if I am to stay in America. And I vant zo very much to stay here. So I vork hard, like she insist, to make certain I reach zese goals.'

Laredo looked dubiously at Heinie. 'This on the level?'

'Ya, ya. Much on level.'

Laredo shook his head in disbelief.

'Zis is how I make sure of my Gerda's future,' Heinie continued, 'while at zer same time keep my secret hidden. But deep inside me, vere a man's conscience lives, I am lazy and owe all my success to my vife.'

''Be damned,' Laredo said. 'I never would've believed it.'

Now, as he stood at the counter paying Heinie for the supplies he'd purchased, Laredo remembered their private conversation, and his gaze strayed to Gerda, who was stocking shelves with new goods. She was several aisles away and he had to squint to see her clearly, but as he watched her he couldn't help admiring the big, buxom Prussian woman for being so supportive of her husband while never taking any of the credit she deserved.

'I figured I'd find you here,' a voice said.

Turning, Laredo saw the young cowboy, a bandage around his head, standing nearby.

'What the hell you doing here?'

Laredo demanded. 'You're supposed to be in bed.'

'That's pure hog slop,' the young cowboy said. 'I don't need to be in bed no more than you do.'

'That's not what Doc Sheldon told me.'

'Told me the same thing, mister. But he ain't fooling me. Goddamn charlatan, he's just trying to soak me for the pills he's forcing me to swallow. But I'm onto him!'

''Onto him'?'

'Sure. When he wasn't looking I chewed one of them pills. Turns out they ain't nothing but schoolmarm's chalk!'

'Chalk, huh?'

'Damned right. You only got to taste 'em to know what they are.'

Laredo eyed him sourly. 'Know much about doctoring, do you?'

'Enough to know what chalk tastes like.'

Laredo, without thinking, punched the young cowboy in the belly, doubling him over in pain. ''Case you're wondering, sonny, that's for talking ill about Doc. There's no finer or more honorable man in all of Brownsville than Jim Sheldon.'

'Says who?' the youth gasped.

'Says everyone,' Laredo said. 'And if you had half the brain of a one-eyed maggot, you'd know what sort of fella he was just by the respect in everyone's voice when his name is mentioned.'

'Mister, vat zis gentleman zay is true,' Heinie assured the young cowboy. 'Dr. Jim, he not only best doctor I ever know, but he most generous one too. Many times he deliver baby for free and no charge patients for making zem vell again. Zo you please desist vid zer bad vords about him or leave my store!'

'You heard him,' Laredo added. 'Make tracks!'

The young cowboy eyed Laredo as if thinking of challenging him, and then decided against it.

'I ain't forgetting this,' he warned hollowly. 'Or you.'

'That was my intention,' Laredo said.

'I still mean to kill you, don't think I don't.'

'Just so long as you don't talk me to death. Now, get moving.'

When the young cowboy still didn't move, Laredo took a threatening step toward him, fists cocked, and the youth quickly turned and staggered out.

Heinie watched him leave. 'It is zer infernal heat,' he said. 'It makes everyone, even my beloved Gerda, bad-tempered.'

'Hopefully he'll learn,' Laredo said. 'But I wouldn't make a bet on it.'

'Give him time, *mein lieber Freund*. Right now he is at zer age ven his mouth talk before his mind veigh consequence.'

'That's a dangerous combination,' Laredo said, ''specially when you malign a man like Doc Sheldon. Hell, 'round here that could get a fella's wings clipped permanently.'

10

That afternoon, as Laredo rode toward the Brownsville-Matamoros Ferry, he sensed he was being followed. He ignored the feeling for a while and then, when it persisted, reined up behind a low mound of rocks. Dismounting, he grabbed his Winchester, scrambled halfway up the rocks and took cover. From here, if he squinted, he could see the dirt trail for a hundred yards or so before it entered the outskirts of town.

He waited, trying to ignore the mosquitoes swarming around him. The insects infested the muddy riverbanks and Laredo, despite swatting them away with his hat, was bitten repeatedly. It was over-hot, the glare bouncing off the rocks adding to the intense temperature. Sweat poured off him and down between his shoulder blades. He desperately wanted a cigarette but held off, concerned that the smoke might betray his position. And when his craving got the better of him, he satisfied it with a handful of Redman, which he stuffed into his cheek and chewed, the juices from the loose-leaf tobacco moistening his dry throat.

A half-hour passed. The sun sank lower. It was now almost in his face, temporarily blinding him. He was forced to pull his hat down over his eyes in order to make out the trail as it snaked toward the sunbaked buildings at the edge of town.

Another ten minutes dragged by, and Laredo was beginning to think he'd made a mistake about being followed — when suddenly a movement caught his attention. He squinted and was able to make out a rider approaching. He was still too far away to recognize, but instinct told Laredo it was the young cowboy. He hoped it wasn't, knowing that if the youth was serious about his threats, he'd have no choice but to kill him.

Normally, the thought of killing a man who was intent on killing him wouldn't have bothered Laredo. But, for some reason that eluded him, he'd let this young man get under his skin, and gunning him down wasn't an option. Angry with himself, Laredo watched the rider drawing closer, all the while trying to figure out how to shake loose from the determined youth, or at least find a way to change his mind without having to shoot him.

A solution didn't come to Laredo until the young cowboy was almost level with him; and then, once it did, it seemed so simple and practical he almost laughed. 'Hold it right there!' he called out. Then, as the young cowboy reined up: 'Keep your hands where I can see 'em. And no sudden moves.' He stepped from behind the rocks, rifle aimed at the youth who studied him with a cocky, slightly contemptuous sneer.

'I knew you was there,' he said as Laredo descended from the rocks.

'Knew it sure as bees make honey.'

'That so?'

'Sure.'

'Yet you didn't shoot me? That was mighty considerate of you.'

'Bushwhacking ain't my style, mister. When I kill a man I like to look him straight in the eye.'

It sounded like a line out of one of Ned Buntline's melodramatic dime novels and Laredo had a hard time not grinning.

'Reckon I'm real lucky then,' he said soberly. 'Not too many fellas place that much importance on integrity.'

'A man's word is all he's got and all he'll be judged by when he passes on,' the youth said, obviously quoting someone.

'Who told you that? Your Pa?'

'Who said anyone told me?'

'Seems like I've heard it before — or some version of it.'

'My Uncle Ellis,' admitted the youth. 'But he didn't hear it from nobody. Swore he made it up himself.'

'Well, either way it's sound advice,' said Laredo. 'Trouble is, it's a hard code to live by. In all my years I never met a man yet who didn't lose sight of the trail now and then.'

The young cowboy's lips tightened into a thin white line. 'That include me, mister?'

Laredo shrugged. ''Fore I can answer that, son, I'd have to know you better. Could be you're that one fella I've been waiting to meet; then again, could be your soul's as crooked as a — ' He broke off as the youth did something he hadn't expected.

He went for his gun.

He was fast; much faster than Laredo expected. Even so, he still had time to swing his rifle like a club and knock the young cowboy out of the saddle. His gun went flying and he landed hard on his back. He lay there for a moment, winded, and then slowly got up and glared at Laredo.

'Damn you, mister,' he raged. 'What's it going to take to make you face me like a man and slap leather?'

'Hopefully, we'll never have to find out,' Laredo said affably.

'You can't duck me forever, mister.'

'I'm not trying to duck you, young fella.'

'Sure looks that way to me.'

'That's 'cause your thinking's all mixed up. If it wasn't, you'd ask yourself why I didn't kill you just now — like I would've if it'd been anyone else dogging my trail.'

Frowning, the youth said: 'So, why didn't you?'

''Cause I got other plans for us.'

'Us?'

'Yeah.' Laredo opened his jacket to show a Deputy U.S. Marshal's badge pinned on his shirt. 'I've just been sworn in, with orders to hunt someone down.'

'Who?'

'An outlaw named Nix.'

'*Carson Nix?*'

'He's the one. Reckon you've heard of him?'

'Who ain't? They say he's killed enough lawmen to fill Boot Hill.'

'That's exactly why I figured I could use some help to arrest him.'

The youth looked incredulously at Laredo. 'You asking me to partner up with you?'

'Just till we arrest or shoot Nix, yeah. I'll have to deputize you, of course, in order to make things legal. But first I need to know if you're up to it.'

The young cowboy answered by removing his hat, showing that the scabby wound on his temple was no longer bandaged.

'Satisfied?'

Laredo nodded. 'So, are you interested in helping me?'

'Depends.'

'On what?'

'What if this Nix fella don't want to be arrested and goes for his iron?'

'Then I'll have no choice but to kill him.'

The young cowboy mulled over Laredo's words, but didn't say anything.

''Course, if you don't have the sand for killing, just say the word. I'll understand.'

'Oh, I got the sand, mister. Don't you worry none about that.'

'Then what's the problem?'

'The reward . . . '

'What about it?'

'I'm wondering if it's worth risking my neck for. How much is it anyway?'

'Whatever it is,' Laredo said, 'it's all yours.'

'No split?'

'Nope. Now, you in or not?'

'This Nix fella — you know where he's holed up?'

''Cross the river in Matamoros, last I heard.'

'And if we find him — bring him in dead or alive — the reward's definitely all mine?'

'Every last cent. Interested?'

'Sure. Count me in.'

'Fair enough.' Laredo extended his hand. 'Name's Laredo Judson.'

'Mine's Willard, Willard Bronson,'

the youth said, shaking hands. 'But everybody calls me Will.'

'Will it is,' said Laredo. 'Now, if you're ready, let's get started. With any luck we can put a few miles between us and the ferry by nightfall.' Without another word they mounted their horses and rode toward the ferry.

11

It wasn't much of a ferry. But then, at that particular crossing point, the Rio Grande wasn't much of a river. Even at high tide, most men could throw a pebble across it. Now, at low tide, the opposite bank, which was Mexican soil, looked 'close enough to spit on,' as the locals were fond of saying. No one said it anymore, but there was a time, Laredo remembered, when the Mexicans found the phrase offensive, feeling that the 'gringos' actually meant they were spitting on them or Mexico itself. But as more work became available in the *Estados Unidos*, and the Mexicans found themselves well-treated by their *Yanqui* bosses, their animosity gradually lessened and relationships between the two peoples greatly improved.

Laredo and Will rode between the trees and bushes growing alongside the river. On reaching the actual bank, they dismounted at the entrance to a narrow plank walk that sloped down to the ferry boats. It was a new addition that Laredo hadn't seen before, and was only there, he guessed, because the locals had complained about walking through the ankle-deep mud that separated them from the little wooden dock.

The grullo hadn't seen the walkway before, either. Skittish and afraid of everything, especially anything new, the horse balked when Laredo tried to lead it down the planking. And when he dragged on the reins, the grullo first tried to bite him and then unexpectedly reared up. Accustomed though he was to the horse's irascibility, Laredo was caught off-guard and almost pulled off the walkway into the mud.

Cursing the animal, Laredo told Will to go ahead, adding: 'Maybe if the sonofabitch sees your roan doing it, he won't be so damned scared and I'll be able to get him down to the dock.'

Will obeyed.

Laredo waited for him to get halfway down the walkway. He then tied his jacket over the grullo's eyes and slowly led the horse after Will. The ploy worked. The grullo cautiously allowed Laredo to lead it down to the dock.

'How come you don't sell that dumb brute and buy one that's more manageable?' Will asked.

'I'd be happy to,' Laredo grumbled. 'But the word's already out 'bout how difficult he is and nobody'll buy the goddamn beast!'

The grullo, as if knowing it was being slighted, cow-kicked, narrowly missing Laredo, who jumped back and then slapped the horse with his hat. 'Damn you, behave yourself!'

Will chuckled but, seeing the scowl on Laredo's face, didn't say anything. Ahead, the passengers on foot had already paid the ferry master and were climbing into two of the four rowboats.

Laredo and Will, the only passengers with horses, stood waiting for the ferry master to motion them forward. Beside them, a sign nailed to one of the posts supporting the roof of the dock displayed the oneway prices to cross the Rio Grande:

5 CENTS PER PERSON.
5 CENTS PER HORSE.
10 CENTS PER WAGON,
LOADED OR EMPTY.

Rowboats took the people across, and a flat-bottomed barge with railings on both sides handled the horses and wagons. Five men hauled the barge, while one oarsman rowed each rowboat across.

Laredo paid the ferryman twenty cents and, because of the grullo's unpredictable behavior, decided to stay with the horses. Will started to join him, then noticed an empty seat beside a pretty girl in the first rowboat, and quickly changed his mind.

'See you on the other side, partner,' he said, and was gone before Laredo could argue. Laredo boarded the barge and stood at the rail beside the grullo. He turned to watch Will, who was hurrying to the first rowboat. Before he reached it, a woman took the seat beside the girl, leaving him no choice but to grab the last seat in the second boat. Laredo had to laugh. Will's companions were two overweight women. They took up most of the seat and Will was barely able to squeeze between them.

The ferryman blew his whistle and the men started hauling the barge across. Laredo grinned and waved at Will, who angrily tried to give him the finger but was unable to raise his trapped arms.

It didn't take long to cross because the river was narrow, shallow and slow-moving. Although the rowboats started after the barge, they reached the other bank first and Will, only too glad to escape his human imprisonment, jumped out as soon as the boat touched the dock. Stretching the stiffness from his cramped body, he stood on the dock to await the approaching barge.

'Next time you see me 'bout to do something dumb,' he said, as Laredo led the grullo and Will's placid red roan ashore, 'kick me, okay?'

'Be glad to,' Laredo said. 'But from what I've seen in the short time I've known you, I ain't sure I got that many kicks in me.' As he was talking, out of the corner of his eye he saw the grullo's hind leg twitch and automatically jumped back, narrowly avoiding the vicious cow-kick that an instant later came his way.

Will shook his head in disbelief. 'Talk about being dumb,' he said. 'How many times do you got to be kicked or bit 'fore you realize that that horse ain't worth the water it drinks?'

Laredo eyed the grullo and shrugged. 'First off, *amigo*, there ain't a horse in all of Texas can run as fast or as far as Cisco. Secondly, he ain't never kicked me — or bit me, for that matter. I'm too savvy for him. And lastly, having to be on my toes all the time is what's kept me alive up till now.'

'What d'you mean?'

'Reflexes,' Laredo said. 'I may be pushing forty, but I got the reflexes of a mongoose.'

'A what?'

'Mongoose. It's a squirrel-like animal that lives in India and Africa someplace. I seen one once in a zoo in St. Louis. Zoo keeper told me it kills snakes. You know, poisonous ones like cobras and black mambas? Stands in front of 'em, daring the snake to strike. Then, when it does, this mongoose fella, he jumps out of the way, grabs the snake behind the head and shakes it till it's dead.'

'Serious?'

Laredo nodded. 'Amazing little critter.'

'What's more amazing,' said Will, impressed, 'is that you know so much for someone who isn't a schoolteacher.'

Laredo shrugged off the compliment. 'It ain't on account of brains,' he assured. 'It comes from having no roots and moving around a lot. Seeing different places and talking to folks smarter than me.'

Will wasn't listening. 'This mongoose,' he said after a little, 'you reckon it could kill a diamondback?'

'It's a snake, ain't it, so I 'spect so.'

Will considered Laredo's answer for a moment before saying: 'Well, I'm not calling you a liar, you understand, but I'd have to actually see you kill a rattler without getting bit 'fore I could believe you.'

'Fair enough. Next time we come across one in the desert, I'll prove it to you. In the meantime,' Laredo added, 'we got another kind of snake to hunt down. So let's get mounted and make some dust.'

12

Matamoros, if nothing else, was a survivor. Discovered by Captain Alonso Alvarez de Pineda in 1519, the same year that Hernan Cortes landed at Vera Cruz, over the centuries the former pueblo had fluctuated in size several times.

Originally a sleepy little border town whose lack of shipping made it unworthy of being called a port, it owed its growth and prosperity to the Civil War, the burgeoning cotton trade, and its close proximity to Texas. But fame and prosperity didn't last. Once the Confederacy collapsed, the bustling port lost its importance and returned to being a sleepy little border town. Adding to its troubles, during the ensuing twenty-odd years, several devastating hurricanes had leveled the area, killing whole families and driving others away, preventing Matamoros from recovering. Lawlessness followed making the town attractive to renegades from both sides of the river, until now it was considered to be one of the most dangerous places in all of Mexico.

Although there were plenty of *gringos* in Matamoros, new ones always aroused suspicion. As Laredo and Will rode along the main street between rows of adobe dwellings, stores and cantinas, everyone they passed gave them suspicious glances.

'Looks like we ain't exactly popular down here,' Will joked. 'And since I've never been here before, it must be you these folks are eyeballing.'

'I've made some enemies here over the years,' Laredo admitted.

'That include jealous husbands?'

Laredo grinned. 'A few, I reckon. 'Course, I wasn't married in them days, so any *Chiquita* wearing a skirt seemed like fair game.'

Will chuckled. 'So it's safe to say that

you and this town ain't exactly strangers?'

Laredo shook his head and said a bit wistfully: 'I've crossed the Rio Bravo more times than I can count.'

'As a lawman or just a randy cowboy looking to chase the rabbit?'

'Both,' Laredo said. 'Till I got married and settled down, that is. After that, only when I was wearing a tin star.' They rode on in silence for a few moments before he added: 'Outlaws figure they're safe once they've crossed the border. And legally, they're right.'

'But you never saw it that way?'

'Nope. A renegade who robs a bank or kills someone is still a renegade no matter what soil he's standing on. 'Least, he is to me.'

'So I've heard,' Will said.

'Meaning?'

'Well, no offense, but you ain't exactly famous for bringing your prisoners in alive.'

Laredo shrugged indifferently. 'I leave that choice up to them.'

'Mean every one of 'em tries to escape?'

'Pretty much. And when they do, you either got to let him go or shoot him. Me, I choose to shoot.'

'I heard that you choose to shoot' whether they tried to escape or not.'

Laredo eyed him shrewdly for a moment. 'Son,' he said softly, 'we're partners and I respect that. We're also both on the same side of the law, and I respect that too.'

'But?'

'There are places in a man's life where even partners shouldn't tread.'

'And if they do?'

'They must pay the price. It's sort of like trespassing,' Laredo continued. 'And in my world, a fella who knowingly trespasses, well, he not only don't deserve to be respected, he's given up his rights to living.'

'In other words,' Will said, 'either I close my yap or you'll shoot me?'

'You catch on fast,' Laredo said, adding with a faint smile: 'Maybe there's hope for you yet, partner.'

Will grinned ruefully and clapped his hands once.

Laredo frowned. 'What're you doing?'

'Closing the vault door on our conversation — *partner!*' They rode on in silence.

Ahead, about halfway down the street was a seedy little cantina called *La Rana Purpura*. Raucous drunken laughter could be heard inside, while gathered outside by an old, chipped statue of a purple frog were several fat, sorry-looking whores who lewdly propositioned every man who passed.

Opposite the cantina, on the corner, stood a tiny rundown church with a broken cross atop its spire, and a mud-spattered wooden sign over its battered door bearing the words: *Iglesia Celestial*. There was nothing heavenly about its appearance. Once pristine white and the pride of Matamoros, it was now in ruins. Rocks and garbage hurled by former disenchanted members, along with hurricanes and endless dust storms, had broken all the windows and worn away most of the paint, leaving the crumbling adobe walls a dirty, muddy brown.

Riding on around in back of the church, Laredo dismounted, handed his reins to Will and told him to stay with the horses.

'Do I have to?' Will challenged. 'I got me a powerful thirst.'

'Me too,' Laredo said. 'And when I finish my business here, I'll buy us both the tallest beer you can lift. Meanwhile, stay put till I get back.' Glancing around to make sure that no one was watching him, he ducked into the rear door of the desecrated church.

13

Inside, the church was in a similar, if not worse, state of decay. Dirt and dust covered everything, cobwebs hung from the overhead beams like the devil's tapestry, and most of the chancel and the altar were damaged. The nave was no different: row after row of pews were in disrepair.

Laredo gazed sadly about him, remembering as he did how peaceful and beautiful the church had been when as a half-starved, terrified, just-orphaned child he'd first seen it after wandering for almost three days and nights in the hot, desolate Mexican desert.

The only child of migrant dirt-farmers, he'd never seen the inside of a church before. But driven by hunger and thirst, and the hope that the band of howling, war-painted Comanches who had slaughtered his folks and the two other families traveling with them wouldn't find him hiding there, he'd timidly entered.

Once inside, he'd immediately felt safe, as if in a candle-lit sanctuary. Too exhausted to even think, he'd crawled under the nearest pew, curled up and promptly fallen asleep. The next thing he remembered was being awakened by a gentle-faced, smiling padre in a brown robe with a crucifix dangling from his neck, offering him a still-warm tortilla . . .

Now, Laredo paused in the aisle, his back to the altar, and looked at that same pew and realized how different his life might have been if Father Delgado hadn't taken him in — Shuffling footsteps chased away his memories. Turning, he saw an old padre in a threadbare robe approaching from the door leading to his quarters. He presented such a pitiful, disconcerting image that momentarily Laredo didn't recognize him. No longer tall, erect or spiritual-looking, he had allowed a loss of hope and too much tequila to break his spirit and turn him into a gaunt, hunched-over skeletal figure devoid of that most important of human traits: dignity. Straggly wisps of white hair sprouted from his once-shaved head, and his dirty, unkempt beard was so long it partly covered the silver crucifix hanging around his neck. Worse, his once-brave and hopeful brown eyes had lost their religious fervor and now reflected years of dissipation and defeat.

A flicker of recognition lit up his leathery, wrinkled face as he saw Laredo. Then, embarrassed by his filthy appearance, he turned away and started back to his quarters.

'Wait!' Laredo called out.

Grudgingly, the old padre stopped, but remained turned away.

'Since when do two old friends not greet each other cordially?'

The old padre flinched as if struck, but didn't answer.

'What happened to the manners you

once taught me — manners you believed were so important that daily you beat them into me with a switch?'

The old padre grew watery-eyed. Turning, he confronted Laredo, saying, 'Forgive me, my son — ' and then stopped, voice choked with emotion.

'For what?' Laredo asked.

Tears rolled down the priest's craggy, dissipated face. 'It is not something I am ready to discuss yet — not even with you, *mi hijo*. All I can ask is: can you possibly imagine how ashamed I am for allowing you to see me like this?'

'How you look don't bother me,' Laredo said. 'I was taught not to judge a man by his appearance, but by his soul . . . and compassion.'

Father Francisco Delgado smiled through his tears. 'You remember my sermons well, my son.'

'I remember your switch more,' Laredo said wryly. Then after they'd both laughed, he added guiltily: 'Forgive me for staying away so long, old friend, but last I heard you had died.'

'From an overabundance of tequila, no doubt?'

Laredo's stony-faced silence told the priest he was right.

'Sadly, I am not that blessed.'

'Coming from you, Father, those are mighty strange words.'

'I am no longer the man you once knew,' Father Delgado said dejectedly. 'Surely you can see that?'

'What I see,' Laredo said, 'is a man in need of repair, much like this church. Nothing more.'

'That is because you cannot see into my soul. If you could, you'd see only a broken spirit, a soul beyond repair.'

'No one's soul is beyond repair. You should know that better than anyone, Father, after all the souls you've repaired. Mine included.'

'I saved your life, *mi hijo*, not your soul.'

'One and the same, ain't they?'

'I fear not. When, as a child, you wandered into this church, your body was in dire need of nourishment, but your soul was pure. It did not need repairing.'

'I can remember when yours was just as pure.'

'I doubt that, my son. But even if it were true, it matters not.' Father Delgado paused, battling inner demons, then said: 'All that matters is that after the Good Lord welcomed me into His arms, I chose to betray His faith in me, to spit in His face by sinning in the most degrading way.'

'What way was that?' demanded Laredo. 'What the hell did you do that caused you to quit on yourself?'

Father Delgado ignored the question, said only: 'Now only death can restore God's faith in me and make my soul pure again.'

'Knowing how you exaggerate, I don't believe that for a second,' Laredo said. 'But even if I did, death is God's call, not yours. Taking your own life is a sin, and the soul of anyone who does it will — and these are your words, Father — rot in hell forever!'

'I do not deny this. But there is no evil in praying to God to take back what He bestowed upon me to begin with.'

Laredo frowned. 'Let me get this straight,' he said. 'You're praying for Him to kill you?'

''Kill' is a harsh word,' Father Delgado said. 'I prefer to think that dying is merely a way of being embraced by God.'

'Call it whatever you like,' Laredo said. 'At the end of the trail you're still dead.'

'I am saved, *mi hijo*. For with death comes everlasting peace, my son.'

'You hope,' Laredo said doubtfully. 'I mean, no one's ever come back and confirmed it.'

Father Delgado wasn't listening. 'But despite my prayers, He chooses not to hear me.'

'You ain't alone,' began Laredo. 'Hell, there was a time when I got so frustrated — '

Father Delgado cut him off. '*Dios mio*,' he said miserably, 'what more can

I do? Every day after penance I beg Him to take me while I am sleeping, only to awake the next morning to face another day of condemnation and abject misery.'

'I know that feeling well,' Laredo said. 'But, like with you, your so-called benevolent God chose not to hear me either — '

'He is not my God, *mi hijo*. He belongs to everyone — including you.'

'Not anymore He don't!' Laredo said. 'No God I'd bend a knee for would let renegades rape and torture my wife and daughter — two of the most gentle, loving souls who ever lived — until they no longer had the strength to beg for mercy. No, let me finish,' Laredo said as the priest started to interrupt. 'It's time I got this off my chest . . . and what better place to do it than in this hellhole that was once a House of Worship?'

Father Delgado again started to protest, but again Laredo cut him off.

'What I'm trying to say,' Laredo

continued, 'is that after they were dead, I did my own share of praying to die.'

'You, *mi hijo*?'

'Don't sound so surprised. I'm human too — even though the scum I've killed would argue that.'

'Yet despite this desire to die,' Father Delgado said, 'you are still here, standing before me?'

'Damn right I am. And here I intend to stay — no matter what the Man Upstairs throws at me.'

'Your decision does not surprise me, *mi hijo*.'

'Then why do your eyes question me?'

'Because I am interested to know how you came to it.'

'I didn't. It came to me. One day, when I was so depressed not even whiskey could deaden the pain, I knew I'd reached rock-bottom. That's when it came to me: a tiny voice inside my head saying I could be drunk and miserable for the rest of my life, or climb out of the bottle, back into the saddle, and go on like destiny intended. The choice was mine.'

'So you chose to live? Why?'

'It was a matter of facing the truth. Survive or eat a bullet. And, miserable as I was, taking the short way home didn't seem like the right choice.'

'It never is, my son.' Father Delgado absently touched the silver crucifix hanging around his neck, then said: 'And now you are here, standing before me as of old, and I am wondering what it is that you need of me.'

'Help, as usual,' Laredo said, adding: 'I'm chasing a killer named Carson Nix.'

'I have heard this name,' Father Delgado said, fingering his dirty, matted white beard. 'He is a man who is said to be of a most vicious nature.'

'Worse than a cornered rat. Do you know where he is?'

'No. But if he is on this side of the Rio Bravo, I am sure I can find out for you. But first, tell me where you are staying, so when the time comes I may contact you.'

'You ain't to contact me at all,' Laredo said. 'Fact is, Father, I don't want you to even speak to me should we happen to cross paths on the street.'

'But — '

'No, no, that's the way it's got to be,' Laredo insisted. 'If Nix was to ever find out you helped me, he'd kill you . . . slowly . . . in a mean, sadistic way not even a Comanche would consider.'

Father Delgado frowned. 'But if we are not to meet, how am I to get word to you?'

'You leave that up to me,' Laredo said, adding: 'Now, I better go. I got me a young colt outside full of piss 'n' beans who's dying of thirst. I'm going to buy him a few tall ones and then I'll figure out where we're going to hunker down for the night.'

'Very well.' Father Delgado smiled fondly and gently kissed Laredo on the forehead. '*Via con Dios, mi hijo.*'

Laredo started to say that God

wasn't going anywhere with him, then decided not to aggravate the old priest, who obviously had enough troubles of his own, and said instead: 'Be of good health, Father.' Turning, he walked to the door, where he paused and gave his friend and mentor a respectful nod before going out.

14

Outside, the horses were gone. So was Will. Instinctively, Laredo dropped his hand to his six-gun and looked around for any signs of danger. There weren't any. All was quiet and still. Puzzled for a moment, Laredo then remembered Will's need of a drink, not to mention the young cowboy's irresponsible nature, and looked at the cantina across the street.

There were several horses tied up outside. Laredo had to squint to see them clearly, and at once saw his grullo and Will's red roan among them.

Angrily, Laredo wondered if he wouldn't be better off by ditching the young cowboy and going after Nix on his own. For a moment he seriously considered it. But then his strange, almost-fatherly feelings for Will resurfaced and, grudgingly fighting down his anger, he crossed the street to the Purple Frog.

Pausing at the entrance, he peered over the batwing doors and saw Will drinking with several tough-looking gunmen at the bar. Alongside these hardcore killers Will looked even younger and more boyishly innocent than usual. Yet, Laredo had to admit, the lawless gunmen not only seemed to have accepted the young cowboy but were actually enjoying his company.

Deciding to find out what was going on, Laredo entered the cantina and approached the bar. He'd intended to eavesdrop on their conversation for a few minutes before joining Will, but his youthful partner spotted him almost immediately and, breaking into a big grin, waved him over.

'Before you yell at me for not doing like you asked,' Will said as Laredo joined him, ''least hear my side of it.'

'Go ahead,' Laredo said. 'I'd like to hear what part of 'stay put till I get back' you didn't understand.'

'It wasn't a question of not under-standing,' Will explained. 'It's just that I came up with a great idea, and figured since you weren't interested in letting me in on whatever it was you were doing in that old church, I'd go ahead and see if it worked.'

'And this idea,' said Laredo, intrigued, 'did it work?'

'Like a charm!' Will turned to the gunmen drinking beside him. 'Didn't it, boys?'

'You bet,' one of them said, while the others all nodded emphatically.

'See?' Will said, grinning. 'Everybody agrees with me.'

'Then maybe you'd be kind enough to tell me,' Laredo said, 'so I can agree too.'

'Be happy to,' Will replied. 'It wasn't nothing you wouldn't have thought of in time, or anything. It just happened to come to me first, that's all.'

'*What* came to you?'

'This idea. I remembered what you told me, how it may take a while to find

Carson Nix, so I figured I'd speed things up by offering a reward.'

'Reward?'

'Five hundred dollars,' put in one of the gunmen. 'Guaranteed, right, boy?' he added to Will.

'Damn right,' Will said. 'Soon as Nix is in custody, I'll have the bank in Philadelphia wire the money to me in Brownsville, and then I'll hand it over to whoever helped us track him down. Fair enough?'

All the gunmen nodded enthusiastically and went back to their drinking.

Will drained his glass and signaled to the bartender to pour two more beers. 'You don't mind me buying you a tall one, do you, partner?' he said to Laredo. 'After all that time you spent in the church, you must be thirsty as hell!'

Laredo, not trusting himself to answer, grabbed Will by the arm and pulled him to one of the tables along the wall. There, he pushed him into a chair and sat across from him.

'Listen,' he said grimly. 'I don't know

what kind of crazy game you're playing, sonny, but offering a reward that you can't pay will end up buying you a wooden box.'

'What do you mean, 'can't pay'?' Will said indignantly. 'Hell, I got almost that much money hid inside my hat. I just figured it mightn't be too smart to mention it to these fellas in case they decided to put a bullet in me and take it for themselves.'

Laredo, not sure how to respond, took a deep breath and tried to stay calm.

'You. Actually. Have. Four. Hundred. Dollars?'

'Four hundred and ten, to be precise, yeah. I'll show it to you if you like.'

'That ain't necessary,' Laredo said. Then, after another deep breath: 'How come a drifter like you, still wet behind the ears, managed to get his hands on that much money?'

Will waited until the bartender had set two tall frothy beers before them and then returned behind the bar before answering. Then, as if embarrassed by what he was about to say, said: 'I guess it's time I told you something.'

Laredo waited silently as Will paused, his look of concern suggesting he was genuinely worried about revealing the truth.

'I'm no drifter,' Will suddenly blurted. ''Least not like you think.'

'Go on,' Laredo said as Will again paused uncomfortably.

'Fact is, partner, I'm only drifting because I don't want my father to find out where I am.'

'Why not?'

'Because if he — or the Pinks — '

'Pinkertons, you mean?'

Will nodded. 'Father hired them to find me. Which they almost did a couple times, once in Dallas and another time in Waco. Fortunately, I eluded them. But they're pros and hard to dodge, and sooner or later my luck's going to run out.'

Sensing that Will was telling the

truth, Laredo said: 'What happens when they do catch up with you?'

'They'll make me go back home. And that's something I surely don't want to do.'

He sounded so serious, so alarmed at the idea of being caught, that Laredo almost felt sorry for him.

'Look,' he said, 'you know I ain't one to stick my nose in another man's business. But you got me downright curious. So I'll risk it this one time and ask you, what's so terrible at home that made you run away from it?'

'That's simple,' Will replied. 'My father.'

'What about him?'

'He'll force me to be a banker, like him.'

Laredo frowned, as if he'd missed something. 'A banker?'

'Yeah.'

'What's so bad about being a banker?'

'You obviously haven't been one, or you'd know,' Will said dejectedly.

'You're right about that,' Laredo admitted. 'But the last banker I saw didn't look like he was suffering too much. Fact is, I kind of envied him. He was Sunday-go-to-church fat, wore a mighty fine suit that most likely cost more than my horse, had a gold watch with a long chain that hung 'cross his belly and was puffing on a dollar cigar long as my arm.'

'That's a banker all right. Describes my father perfectly.'

'Then what's your problem?'

'I don't want to work in a bank. I want to be . . . '

'Go on.'

'A lawman, like you. Oh, I know you're not rich like Father, or like I will be once the bank becomes mine — '

'Your pa *owns* the bank?' Laredo said, eyebrows arching.

Will nodded. 'Three of them, actually,' he said as if it were a crime. 'Two in Philly and one in Boston. And he's opening a new one soon, in New York, which he wants me to run, and — '

'Hold it,' Laredo said, raising his hand. 'I want your word on something.'

'What?'

'I want you to swear that all you just told me is the truth . . . the real God's truth, I mean. Not just some imagined kind of truth that you've invented to make yourself sound like you're rich.'

'No, no,' Will said emphatically. 'Everything I told you is true. I am rich. Very rich.'

'But you want to be a sheriff or a marshal, right?'

Will nodded. 'More than anything,' he said with such boyish enthusiasm that Laredo could not help but like him. 'That's why I've been dogging you. Everyone says you're the best there is . . . better even than Wyatt Earp, and — well, I was hoping you'd teach me to be just like you.'

Laredo didn't know what to say.

'I know it's a lot to ask,' Will continued. 'But I'm willing to do anything you ask if it'll make you say yes. That's why I thought about putting up a reward for Nix. I figured if I help you catch him, then you might be more willing to keep me on as your deputy. You know. And teach me stuff as we go along.'

Laredo let his feelings out in a long, explosive sigh.

'Would you?' Will pressed. 'If I help you catch Nix, I mean?'

'Well, I ain't making no promises, you understand,' Laredo said. 'But I can't deny that it would go a long way toward encouraging me to keep you on as my deputy.'

'That's all I'm asking for,' Will said, 'a chance. Honestly.'

'But for the moment,' Laredo continued as if Will hadn't spoken, 'let's just see how things play out. Okay?'

'Sure,' Will said, with his usual eagerness. 'Anything you say, Marshal.'

Laredo rolled his eyes.

'To catching Nix,' Will said, raising his glass.

'To catching Nix,' Laredo agreed.

They clinked glasses and drank.

15

That night they made camp in a narrow arroyo just outside of town. Laredo still hadn't gotten over his surprise about Will being the son of a rich banker in Philadelphia, and would have liked to have known more about him. But he wasn't one to pry, and after they built a fire and spread their bedrolls, they sat with their backs against a boulder, smoking hand-rolls and drinking coffee while listening to the coyotes' mournful chorus.

Will broke the silence between them first. 'I'm sorry I didn't tell you who I was before, but being a lawman, I was afraid if you found out I'd run away you might contact the Pinks, or even my father.'

'How do you know I still won't?' Laredo replied. 'I'm sure he'd pay me handsomely if I gave him your whereabouts.'

'So would the Pinks,' Will said. 'Knowing Father, he not only hired them to track me down but promised them a big reward if they found me. I'm sure they'd be happy to split it with you if you saved them months of tedious investigation.'

'In other words, you'd understand if I did?'

'Sure. Or at least I'd try to.'

'But you don't think I will, is that it?'

'I know you won't,' Will said earnestly. 'Now that I've gotten to know you better and seen the kind of man you are, I'd bet my life you wouldn't.'

'That's exactly what you are doing, isn't it — betting your life on me?'

'I suppose so.' Will yawned, drained his cup and threw the coffee dregs off into the darkness. 'Truthfully, I never gave it that much thought.'

Laredo studied the young man sitting across the fire from him, wondering as he did if Will would still trust him if he knew that just a few days ago he was facing a rope. He also wondered what kind of father would want to control his son's future to the extent of forcing him to work at a job that he knew would make him miserable. The pictures he came up with weren't exactly pretty.

It must have showed on his face because Will, after stubbing out his smoke, said: 'He's not really that bad — my father, I mean. It's just that I'm his only son and he wants what he thinks is best for me.'

Laredo shrugged and, trying to sound as if he didn't care one way or another, said: 'Everyone's got their faults.'

'Amen to that.'

Neither of them spoke again for several minutes.

Then Laredo said: 'Your ma — what's she think about all this?'

Will sighed unhappily. 'Mother's dead — died giving birth to me.'

'I'm sorry,' Laredo said, cursing himself for even mentioning it.

'It's all right,' Will said. 'I never knew her, of course, and not having any older brothers or sisters, I've only Father's opinion of her to go by. She was apparently very pretty,' he added after a pause, 'and Father was devoted to her.'

'Sounds like there's a 'but' in there somewhere,' Laredo said.

Will thought for a moment before saying: 'Grampa Ellis — that's my mother's dad — he claims Father bullied her like he bullies everyone else. 'Course, to be fair, that's just his opinion. Other people I've spoken to — my three uncles, for instance — they admit Father dominated her, but say that Mother didn't seem to mind. In fact, she quite enjoyed it. And whenever someone questioned her about it, she'd tell them that all she'd ever wanted in life was to have a great big family and to be taken care of, and Father fitted her needs in both categories.'

'And how 'bout your pa — did he ever remarry?'

Will shook his head. 'He almost did,

on two occasions. But then, according to him — and I've no reason to think he's lying — he backed out at the last minute.'

'Why? Did he ever tell you?'

'Oh, sure. Several times, in fact.' Will smiled ruefully. 'Said he decided it wouldn't be fair on the new wife, whoever she was, because he'd always be comparing her to Mother, and he didn't think anyone could live up to a perfect ghost.'

'That's an odd comment to make.'

'Yeah. I asked him about it once, and he said, what he really meant to say was that because Mother died so young, so soon after they got married, she never had time to fall off the pedestal he put her on ... and no woman, however hard she tried, could hope to compete with that.'

Somewhere off in the darkness a coyote yip-yipped to the moon.

Laredo waited until the mournful yowling ceased, then said: 'Funny thing.'

'What?'

'You been listening to yourself?'

'What do you mean?'

Laredo chuckled. 'Ever since you told me 'bout your pa and how you're rich and all, you been talking differently.'

'Differently?' Will frowned. 'How do you mean?'

'More . . . educated.'

'Oh.' Will paused, then grinned and said: 'Guess now I don't have *any* secrets from you.'

'You didn't need to have any from the get-go.'

'I know that now. And I'm ashamed of myself for trying to make you believe I was someone other than myself.'

'Forget it,' Laredo said. 'I have.'

'Thanks.'

'But from now on . . . '

'Don't worry,' Will assured him. 'From this moment on, anything that comes out of my mouth will be the truth. That, you have my word on.'

'Fair enough.' Laredo ground out his smoke on the heel of his boot before adding: 'Reckon it's time to get some shut-eye. I got a feeling that from now on, we got nothing but long dangerous days ahead of us.'

16

Dawn broke early, the wafer-like sun inching above the distant mountains, its brilliant rays flooding the pale gray sky with spears of color.

As if the sun were his private alarm-clock, Laredo instantly awoke, yawned and rubbed the sleep from his eyes. Inside his bedroll he felt the steely hardness of his Peacemaker pressing against his thigh. The gun reminded him that, despite the tranquility of the heavens above, in the world he lived in there were men anxious to kill him.

It was a sobering thought, one he'd lived with ever since the first day he'd pinned on a sheriff's star, and instinctively he listened to see if he could hear any sounds warning him that danger was closing in on them.

But all was quiet. Not even the coyotes were stirring.

Satisfied all was well, Laredo glanced over at Will.

The youth lay on his back, snuggled comfortably in his bedroll, snoring blissfully.

Laredo rose up on his elbows and studied him. For the second time he considered leaving Will and going after Nix alone. But this time it wasn't because he distrusted Will or felt he was an annoying hindrance; this time it was because he looked so damned innocent Laredo felt guilty for risking the young man's life.

Before he could decide what to do, the need to urinate forced Laredo to climb out of his bedroll and duck behind the nearest boulder. There, with a contented sigh, he relieved himself. As he did, a cold wind blew in from the desert. Shivering, Laredo listened to its faint moaning. Otherwise, save for an occasional snuffling of the horses, it was stone quiet. And as he shook away the last drops and buttoned up his long johns, he wondered where Carson Nix was at that moment, and whether today was the day that one or both of them ended up dead.

When he returned to his bedroll, Laredo saw that the fire had gone out. He pulled on his jeans and boots, then his denim shirt and jacket, and dug in his pocket for matches.

'Save them,' Will said behind him. 'There's got to be one or two hot embers among the ashes that I can use to start a fire.'

Laredo turned and saw Will climbing out of his bedroll.

'Matches are hard to come by,' Will added, joining him. 'I know from experience. Several times I've run out and had to drink cold coffee. And boy, if there's one thing I really detest, it is cold coffee.'

'Go ahead,' Laredo said, moving aside. 'But put a spur to it. I want to check on Father Delgado 'fore the sun gets much higher.'

'Is that who you were talking to inside the church all that time?'

Laredo nodded. 'He's an old and trusted friend . . . someone who helped raise me.'

'Can he help us find Nix? It's all right if you don't want to tell me,' Will added when Laredo didn't answer. 'I don't have to know everything. Not till I prove you can really trust me, anyway. But then — '

'We'll talk about it,' Laredo said. 'Meantime, get the fire started while I dig out the coffee.'

Once the fire was going, they ate strips of jerky fried in a pan and some of the left-over tortillas that Will kept wrapped in his saddlebag. They then washed everything down with two mugs of scalding hot black coffee. Then, bellies full, they saddled up and rode back toward town. By the time they reached the outskirts, dawn had been replaced by a chilling, damp morning mist that cast an eerie shroud over the ruins of the old church.

'Shall I wait here?' Will said as they dismounted by the rear entrance.

'No,' Laredo said. 'I don't want — '

Will stopped him. 'I'll stay put this time, I swear. I mean, the cantina's not open — '

'I ain't worried about you or the cantina,' Laredo said. 'I just don't want folks to know we're here. Nix has friends everywhere. One of 'em might tell him that he saw us here, and then who knows what that twisted sonofabitch would do. He might burn Father Delgado's eyes out just for the goddamn hell of it.'

'Then why don't we take the horses inside?' Will suggested. 'That'll solve everything. No one will see us, and you and the priest can talk for as long as you like.'

Laredo nodded, pleased. 'That's using 'em,' he said.

'What?'

'Your brains.'

'Careful,' Will said drily. 'If I didn't know better, partner, I might mistake that for a compliment.' Before Laredo could respond, Will grabbed both reins and led the horses through a gap in the crumbling walls into the church.

Laredo looked after him for a moment and then shook his head. ''Be damned,' he muttered. 'Could be that boy has the makings of a genuine deputy after all . . . '

17

Laredo found Father Delgado kneeled in prayer beside his cot in his tiny cell-like quarters. There were tiles missing in the damaged roof above him and through the hole a ray of early morning sunlight framed the old padre's head like a halo.

Not wanting to disturb him, Laredo was about to leave, when he heard faint snoring and realized that the priest had fallen asleep while praying. Approaching, Laredo gently shook him by the shoulder. Father Delgado woke and, blinking in the sunlight, looked about him, confused, as if not aware of where he was . . .

'*Esta bien, Padre*,' Laredo said quietly. '*Soy yo . . . Laredo.*'

Recognizing him, Father Delgado smiled and started to rise. His weak, cramped legs buckled and he would have fallen if Laredo hadn't grabbed his arm and steadied him.

'Thank you, *mi hijo*,' he said as Laredo helped him sit on the cot. 'I fear these old legs are betraying me.'

Laredo wasn't fooled. Glancing about him at the stone-walled cell that was devoid of all creature comforts, including food, he said: 'When'd you last eat, Father?'

'Why . . . uh . . . yesterday, I think.'

Laredo, guessing it was more like several yesterdays, looked chidingly at the old, gaunt priest. 'Wait here, Father. Don't move. Be right back.'

Leaving the room, Laredo rejoined Will, who stood with the horses in front of the damaged altar.

'You got any of them tortillas left?'

'S-Sure. A few . . . ' Will frowned, puzzled. 'Why?'

'Give 'em to me,' Laredo said. 'And any jerky, if you got some.'

Will obliged. Then, tying the horses to a broken pew, he followed Laredo to the old priest's quarters. There, Laredo introduced Will as his deputy to Father Delgado, then respectfully but firmly insisted the padre eat the tortillas and jerky.

The old priest obeyed, tears of gratitude moistening his eyes. As he wolfed down the food, he explained that last night he had asked certain people he knew — church-goers whom he trusted implicitly — if they knew the whereabouts of Carson Nix.

'What'd they say, Father?' Will asked impatiently. 'Did they know where he is?'

Laredo shot him a look, warning him to not interrupt, but Father Delgado merely smiled and said: 'Not at this moment, no. But from what they heard, they think they know where he has been for the past few weeks.'

'Where?' Will blurted.

'Dammit, give the man a chance to eat,' Laredo said crossly. Then gently to the old padre: 'Take your time, Father. Eat. Right now, the most important thing is that you get some food into you. Then we can figure out where Nix is.'

Father Delgado smiled. 'Thank you for your concern, *mi hijo*. But I can talk as I eat.' Swallowing the last of the jerky, he added to Will: 'To answer your question, *joven*, my friends believe that Carson Nix has been living with a woman in one of the pueblos south of here. They didn't know which one, but are making inquiries even as we speak.'

'Great,' Will exclaimed. 'Now we're finally getting somewhere.'

'You said 'has',' Laredo said. 'Does that mean Nix is no longer with this woman?'

Father Delgado shrugged his frail shoulders. 'In truth, this I cannot answer. But my friends implied that he and his men have left the village and are now on their way here.'

'Men?'

'This Nix, he has followers, *compadres*.'

'Are you sure? I thought Nix always rode alone.'

'I am sure of nothing,' Father Delgado said. 'Since I do not know this man, I cannot say what is or isn't true. I can only repeat what I was told. Any conclusions you make, *mi hijo*, must come from your own knowledge based upon what my friends say.'

Laredo nodded but kept his thoughts to himself.

Finished eating, Father Delgado picked up an earthen jug from under his cot and drank until it was empty.

'Here, let me have that,' Laredo said. Taking the jug from the priest, he handed it to Will, adding: 'There's a well out back. Fill this up, will you?'

Will nodded and hurried out.

'He's a good boy,' Laredo said to Father Delgado. 'A tad hotheaded, and maybe rash at times, but once he grows into his stirrups, he'll be well worth his salt.'

Father Delgado smiled tolerantly. 'I seem to remember saying something very similar once to another young man.'

'Yeah,' Laredo grunted. 'And look how *he* turned out.'

'In my humble opinion, few men have ever turned out better.'

'Thanks. But we all know you're prejudiced, Father.'

'Indeed I am, *mi hijo*. Prejudiced and most proud.' Before Laredo could respond, Father Delgado added: 'Before we part, there is something I must know. When you find this Nix, do you intend to kill him?'

'That depends on him — whether he surrenders peacefully or puts up a fight.'

'We both know the answer to that, do we not?'

'Then he must take what's coming to him.'

Father Delgado frowned, troubled by his thoughts. 'These rumors I hear,' he said finally, 'the ones that describe the fate of all your captives — are they true?'

'What do *you* think?'

'You know I would never condemn

you until I heard the truth from your own lips.'

Laredo shrugged. 'Well, the truth is, I've shot a lot of them, so I reckon the rumors are mostly true.'

Father Delgado looked displeased, but didn't say anything.

Reading the old priest's expression, Laredo felt obliged to say: 'Don't give me that look, Father. You know as well as I do that when I pinned on this star I swore to uphold the law, no matter how violent the consequences were.'

'Does that include murder?'

'Dammit, I ain't a murderer,' Laredo replied angrily. 'And I won't let anyone call me one either — not even you, Father.'

Stung, Father Delgado fell silent, his eyes downcast.

Ashamed of his flare-up, Laredo softened his tone, saying: 'What no one understands, Father — including you — is that bringing in an outlaw when he knows he's facing prison or a rope is a dangerous, thankless job. They only got one thing on their mind: escape. And depending on the outlaw, how desperate he is and to what lengths he's willing to go not to be brought in, it boils down to survival: my life or his. I know that. He knows that. And though lawmen never talk about it, all of us know that when dealing with renegades it's just a matter of who can kill the other first.' Laredo paused to gather his thoughts, then said: 'Do I sometimes make a mistake — misjudge a fella's intentions and pull the trigger 'fore he can kill me? — sure. I'd never argue that. But so what? These men are scum, worse than the lowest sidewinder, so where's the crime?'

'If you don't know,' Father Delgado said sadly, 'then I have failed you miserably.'

'You ain't failed me,' Laredo insisted. 'Hell, we both know where I'd be today without you, Father, and for that I'll always be indebted to you.'

'That is not necessary,' Father Delgado began — and then stopped as Will returned carrying the jug of water.

'Here you go, padre.' Will set the jug down by the cot. 'I filled it extra full so it'll last you longer.'

'*Gracias*,' Father Delgado said. 'I am most grateful to you.'

From the door Laredo said: 'Remember what I told you, Father. If we should ever meet, no matter where it is, you're to pretend you don't know me. We clear on that?'

'Most clear,' Father Delgado said. 'Hard as that will be, *mi hijo*, I shall do as you ask. But know that my blessings always are with you no matter where you go.'

18

Outside, behind the church, the two of them swung up into their saddles. The mist had now lifted and the morning sun shone brightly in their eyes.

'Where to now?' Will asked.

'You tell me.'

Will eyed Laredo suspiciously. 'You really want to know what I think, or are you just testing me?'

'Either way,' Laredo said, 'I'd like an answer.'

'Well,' Will said, mind churning, 'since we don't know which village Nix's woman lives in, there's no point in wasting our time going from one to another. It not only would wear out our horses, but I doubt if anyone would tell us the truth even if we lucked onto the right one, so — '

'Dammit, get to the meat, will you?' Laredo growled.

'I am, I am. Don't rush me,' Will grumbled. Then: 'Okay, since according to Father Delgado's friends, Nix and his men are riding this way — '

'What if they're not?' Laredo challenged. 'Are you just going to take his or his friends' word for it? If you are, that means you're relying on second- — no, third-hand — information, and — '

'If you'd just shut up and let me finish for once,' Will broke in, 'you'd know that that isn't the only reason I think Nix is coming here.'

'Go ahead,' Laredo said. 'If you got something more to say, let's hear it.'

'The other reason — the more important reason I think Nix is headed this way,' Will continued, 'is because of what Kate told us.'

'Kate?'

'Sure. Remember? She said Nix was sweet on one of her girls. And since he probably doesn't know yet that you've gunned down the Cobb brothers, chances are he and his men are riding

154

this way for a night of fun.'

'Sounds fair enough,' Laredo said. 'So what's your plan?'

'We ambush them.'

'Not me,' Laredo said. 'I don't bushwhack nobody. Not even a weasel like Nix.'

'Who said anything about bush-whacking? By ambushing, I mean we take cover beside the main trail and get the jump on them — force them to throw down their guns.'

'And if they ain't in the mood to surrender?'

'Then we have every legal right as lawmen to shoot them.'

'Every-legal-right? Judas, you sound like a lawyer.'

'That's because two of my uncles are lawyers and they were always cornering me and expounding — '

'Doing what?'

'Expounding. Explaining how the law works in infinite detail. I didn't want to be rude — after all, they are my uncles — so I politely tried to ignore them.

But it never worked. They just kept hammering away.' Will shook his head, frustrated. 'They mean well, you understand. They just can't believe that anyone could find the law dull or boring. I also think they're hoping their vast knowledge of the law will not only impress me, but encourage me to become a lawyer myself.'

'Lawyer? I thought they wanted you to be a banker?'

'That's my father. Uncles Jed and Jim, they want me to go into law. Even offered to pay for law school and then, after I graduated, promised to make me a junior partner at their firm in Boston. 'Course, I turned them down, but . . . it just never seems to sink in that I'm serious. As a result, they never give up . . . which is another reason I ran away. I just couldn't take it any longer.'

Laredo had stopped listening. 'A cowboy lawyer?' he said, thinking aloud. 'Huh, I ain't never heard of one of them.'

'Neither have I,' said Will. 'And I sure

as hell don't intend to become the first.'

Laredo chuckled, despite the grimness of his mood.

'What's so funny?' Will demanded.

'Nothing,' Laredo said.

'Tell me.'

'Well, I was just thinking. In all the years I've been in the saddle, from the time I left Father Delgado to the first time I pinned on a star, riding from here to hell and back, I never met anyone who was so all-fire determined not to become rich or smart. And that's the bare-assed truth of it.'

'You say that like you don't think cowboys or lawmen are smart.'

'Some are, some ain't. Depends on the fella. But I'll tell you this, *amigo*, even the ones who are — like Bat Masterson and John Wesley Hardin, who actually studied law while he was in prison — they're smart in a different way.'

'How do you mean?'

Laredo shrugged. 'It's hard to throw a rope over it, *amigo*. But I'll tell you this: it don't come from books or studying in school, but by learning from your mistakes. That is, of course, if you're lucky enough to make a mistake and life gives you a second chance.'

'I'll remember that,' Will said, pulling the brim of his hat lower over his eyes. 'That way, maybe I can become a famous lawman like you.'

About to deny he was famous, Laredo saw a glint of amusement in his young deputy's eyes and realized Will was jerking his tail. Inwardly, he laughed. Then without a word he dug his spurs in, goading the startled grullo into a smooth, mile-consuming gallop.

'Hey!' Will exclaimed. 'Wait for me.' He spurred his roan after Laredo, who was riding into the sun, following the main trail as it wound its way southeast across the barren wasteland.

19

The Vasquez Rocks were located some three miles southeast of Matamoros. Named after a once-famous local Mexican bandit, the rocks covered the slopes of two low hills that straddled the main trail. Besides all the rocks, each hill was peppered with small caves that offered bandits and outlaws ideal hiding places. Because of this most travelers, afraid of being robbed, refused to pass between the rocky hills and instead rode around them, picking up the trail a safe distance beyond them.

Laredo and Will ignored the potential danger and followed the trail as it curved between Vasquez Rocks. Dismounting about halfway through, they led their horses around behind the smaller and rockier of the two hills. Here, they watered them, hobbled them and left them in the shade of some boulders that hid them from anyone approaching from the south.

The two men then grabbed their rifles, scrambled halfway up the hillside and took cover behind a cluster of rocks overlooking the trail. From here, the view in both directions was visible for as far as they could see. Laredo made sure no one was approaching from either direction, then moved behind a rock, where he couldn't be seen, dug out the fixings and told Will to keep watch while he had a smoke.

Will nodded. Yawning, he leaned back against a rock and settled in to wait.

'Don't get too comfortable,' Laredo warned. 'With my eyes I can't see the trail from here. You fall asleep and — '

'Dammit,' Will exclaimed, 'will you quit treating me like a Goddamn tenderfoot? I swear you're worse than an old maid with her bloomers in a knot.'

'Better knotted bloomers,' Laredo deadpanned, 'than ants in your crotch.'

Will wasn't amused. 'Look,' he said earnestly, 'just for once, will you stop worrying and trust me? I swear I won't let you down. I got eyes like an eagle, and I promise I'll let you know the second I see any riders approaching, all right?'

Laredo grudgingly nodded, and settled back to enjoy his smoke.

Will sighed, grateful for a few minutes of peace and quiet. He leaned back against the rock, the sun warm on his upturned face. Moments later he heard the scratch of a match. He glanced over his shoulder and saw a thin spiral of smoke drifting up from behind the rock hiding Laredo. The sweet smell of tobacco toyed with his senses. He closed his eyes and inhaled deeply to fully enjoy the aroma.

The next thing he remembered was being hit hard in the ribs. He woke with a painful gasp and saw Laredo hunkered down beside him, furious, ready to hit him again with the butt of his Winchester.

'What the hell'd you do that for?' he demanded, rubbing his ribs.

Laredo, teeth gritted, said: 'You're lucky it was your ribs! You deserve to have your skull busted wide open!'

'W-Why? What'd I do?'

Laredo said only: 'It serves me right. I never should've brung you along in the first place. I should've wired the Pinks where you were and collected the reward.'

'It's not too late,' Will said angrily. 'There's a telegraph office 'cross the river in Brownsville. Can wire them from there. Hell, I'll even give you their address in St. Louis. That way you'll get your money faster!'

Laredo hit him. Will's head snapped back from the punch and he went sprawling.

He lay there for a moment, dazed. But this time he didn't stay down. Jumping up, he threw himself at Laredo. Both men bounced off a rock;

then, still grappling and unable to stop, went rolling and sliding down the slope.

They might have slid all the way to the bottom but for a large boulder blocking their path. Slamming into it, they sat there, winded and dazed, trying to catch their breath, dirt and stones slithering all the way down to the bottom of the hill.

Will recovered first. 'Satisfied?' he demanded.

'No, but it'll have to do,' Laredo said. He winced and gingerly grabbed his side, adding: 'Feels like I busted a rib.'

'Serves you right,' Will grumbled. 'What the hell got into you anyway? I mean, what'd I do to piss you off so badly?'

'Don't pretend you don't know.'

'I don't.'

'Goddammit, you fell asleep!'

'That's a lie. I just closed my eyes for a second — '

'Like hell you did. Look where the sun is,' Laredo said, thumbing skyward.

Will obeyed and saw that the sun was

directly overhead. Surprise then guilt creased his youthful tanned face as he realized that he'd been asleep for at least thirty minutes. He then looked back at Laredo, completely crushed.

'Go ahead,' he said, thrusting out his chin. 'Hit me again. Hit me as many times as you like. I deserve it — that and more. I mean it,' he added when Laredo didn't move. 'Pound on me all you want. It won't make up for me letting you down, but — '

'Shut up!' Laredo said suddenly, looking off.

'What?'

'I said, shut up! And keep down!' He pressed Will to the dirt with one boot and continued to squint off into the distance.

'Riders?'

Laredo nodded. 'They're still pretty far off, so they may not have seen us.'

'Is it Nix?'

'Could be. I can't see 'em real good, but I think I recognize his horse. It's a gray with dark blotches on its rump

— like an Appaloosa.'

'Let me look,' Will said. 'There's nothing wrong with my eyes.'

Reluctantly, Laredo removed his boot, saying: 'Okay, but don't get up too far. They probably ain't expecting trouble, but you never know. 'Sides, Nix or one of his men might have field glasses or one of them long telescopes they use at sea.'

Will got to his knees and cautiously peered over the boulder. The heat made the horizon hazy, but in the shimmering waves he made out a group of riders approaching in the distance.

'Well?' Laredo demanded when Will didn't say anything. 'Is it Nix, you think?'

'I can't make out any faces. But if you're right about the gray, yeah. 'Course, it could be someone else riding it — '

'Nobody rides that gray other than Carson Nix,' Laredo said grimly. 'Just ask the two men he shot for getting too close while they were admiring it.'

'He killed two men just for admiring his horse?' Will said incredulously.

'Shot 'em down in cold daylight,' Laredo said, adding: 'Now you know the kind of mud-sucking skunk we're dealing with.' He stared off toward Nix and, thinking aloud, said: 'You know, shooting a fella, no matter whether he deserves it or not, always makes me sick in the belly. But when it comes time to put a slug into Nix, reckon I may just celebrate.'

'The more I hear about him,' Will said, 'I'll join you.'

20

It took Nix and his men forty minutes to reach Vasquez Rocks. By then Laredo and Will had positioned themselves behind two small boulders a short distance up the hill, their rifles trained on the outlaws below.

'Carson Nix!' Laredo shouted as Nix and his five men drew level with him. 'This is Deputy US Marshal Judson! Drop your guns and raise 'em high!' Without revealing himself he fired a single shot, the bullet kicking up dirt a few feet ahead of Nix's horse.

Startled, the leggy gray stallion reared up, snorting, catching Nix off-guard so that he was almost thrown from the saddle. Furious, he finally controlled the horse and, like his men, looked up at the rocks, trying to locate the shooter.

'I ain't going to do nothing till you

show yourself,' he yelled. 'Hell, for all I know you might be trying to rob us!'

'He's right,' chimed in one of the men. 'I want to see your badge 'fore I throw down my guns.'

'Okay,' Laredo replied. 'But I'm warning you: my deputy's got a bead on you, Nix. Any sudden move and he'll put a bullet 'tween your ears!' In a whisper he added to Will: 'Shoot the first sonofabitch who even looks like he's going for his gun.'

'Happy to,' Will said.

Laredo slowly stepped from behind the boulder protecting him, one hand keeping his rifle trained on Nix, the other pulling back his jacket to reveal the Deputy US Marshal's badge pinned to his shirt.

'Satisfied?' he asked Nix.

'Reckon . . . '

'Then do like I say and get rid of them irons. *Pronto*!'

Nix hesitated, and in that moment the man behind him grabbed for his six-gun.

Will fired. The shot knocked the man from his saddle, killing him and startling the other men.

'Anybody else deaf?' Laredo said. Then, as no one answered: 'Good. Now empty your holsters and grab some sky.'

Grudgingly, Nix and the four remaining men threw away their six-guns and raised their hands.

Laredo spoke out the corner of his mouth to Will. 'Don't go getting noble on me just 'cause they're unarmed.'

'Don't worry,' Will said. 'Those days are behind me.'

Laredo scrambled down between the rocks to the trail. Once there, he kept his eyes on Nix while working his way around the men, kicking their guns aside each time he came to one. He then faced Nix and told him to throw down his rope. 'And while you're at it,' he said after Nix had obeyed, 'get rid of that belly gun. Easy!' he added as Nix reached inside his shirt. 'My deputy's dying to make a name for hisself, and shooting you would give his reputation a real boost.'

Nix slowly took out the short-barreled Colt revolver and dropped it on the ground.

'Smart move,' Laredo said. Then to Will: 'You can come down, Deputy. These gents need an escort into town.'

Will gave an acknowledging wave and came slithering down the rocky slope.

'I'll get our horses,' he told Laredo and, without waiting for an answer, hurried off.

Laredo kept his rifle aimed at Nix, ready to squeeze off a round if the outlaw made even the slightest move. But Nix knew better.

'What're you waiting for?' he said. 'We both know you're going to shoot us anyways, so why not get it over with?'

'Don't tempt me,' Laredo warned. 'I'm trying to turn over a new leaf and bring a prisoner in alive for a change. But I wouldn't lose no sleep if I had to shoot you.' He paused as Will reappeared, riding his horse and leading Laredo's.

'Keep 'em covered while I tie their hands,' Laredo said, picking up the rope. 'One of 'em so much as sneezes, take him down.'

'Be my pleasure,' Will said. He drew his Colt, thumbed back the hammer and aimed the gun at Nix. His back was now facing the hillside; and, as Laredo drew his Bowie and started cutting the rope into short lengths, he also had his back to the hill.

Big mistake!

Two hard-eyed bearded gunmen, outlaws who'd been holed up there, stepped out of one of the ground-level caves. Both were armed with rifles, and before either Laredo or Will noticed them, one shot the Colt out of Will's hand while the other fired at Laredo's back.

Laredo would have been dead but for the grullo, which chose that same instant to try to kick him, making him jump back. The bullet intended for Laredo pierced the grullo's neck. The horse squealed and went down, kicking and thrashing in pain.

Simultaneously, Nix and his men wheeled their horses around and spurred them toward Laredo and Will. Two of them slammed into Will's horse, knocking the roan down and sending Will sprawling. Nix and the other men charged straight at Laredo, who fired from the hip. The bullet killed one man. But before Laredo could fire again the horses crashed into him, knocking him to the ground.

As he lay there, momentarily stunned, he heard shooting. It seemed to be coming from far off. Shaking away the cobwebs he rolled over and saw Nix ruthlessly gun down the two bandits who'd been holed up in the cave. Laughing, as if proving there was no honor among thieves, he and his men then rode off.

More shooting followed. Laredo, focused now, turned and saw Will on his knees, firing at Nix and his men as they galloped away.

Laredo grabbed his own gun from the dirt and kept shooting until it was empty. He was firing too quickly to aim, but he still managed to hit the rider nearest Nix. The man slumped over his saddle, life ebbing, and slowly slid from his horse. Nix and the other two men continued riding and were soon out of range.

'Nice shooting,' Will said to Laredo.

'Lousy, you mean. I was aiming at Nix.'

'Either way, it's one less man to deal with when we catch up with Nix. We are going after him, right?' Will added when Laredo didn't answer.

'I am,' Laredo said pointedly.

'What the hell's that supposed to mean?'

'What it sounds like. Look,' he said, seeing Will's disappointment, 'I get paid to take a bullet. You don't.'

'Heard me complaining, have you?'

'No, and I'm real grateful to you for helping me out. But now that I know where Nix is — or will be, once he crosses the river — I don't need your help anymore.'

'Like hell you don't,' Will said. 'We're partners, and partners don't quit on each other in the middle of a job.'

'That's just it, son — this ain't your job.'

'That's not the way I see it. Anyways, job or no job, I'm going with you.'

'No, you ain't,' insisted Laredo. 'And that's an order!' Giving Will no time to argue, Laredo turned and put a bullet in the suffering grullo's brain. The horse stopped thrashing around, gave a final shudder and died. Laredo sighed regretfully and started removing his saddle.

'One thing you can do for me, though,' he said. 'When you reach Matamoros, buy me another horse. Here.' He took money from one of his saddlebags and offered it to Will. 'Pay whatever it takes.'

'Buy your own damn horse!' Will angrily pushed the money aside. He then kicked up his roan and rode back to Matamoros ... leaving Laredo standing in the middle of the trail, saddle at his feet.

21

After Will had ridden a half-mile or so, he cooled off enough to realize he couldn't leave Laredo to walk back to town in the broiling heat; especially while lugging a saddle. He reined up, angry with himself for letting his feelings get the upper hand, and wheeled the roan around. It was then he noticed a saddled horse standing a short distance away. It had belonged to one of the dead outlaws. Reins draped loosely over its neck, the big sorrel stared inquisitively at Will, as if asking him to explain why its master lay in a bloody heap at its feet.

Will nudged his roan toward the horse, talking softly to it in an effort to keep it from running off. The sorrel backed up and shied skittishly as he got close, red coat twitching, eyes filled with fear, but made no attempt to run away.

Dismounting, Will continued to talk softly to the horse, and gradually got close enough to grasp one of the reins. He then grabbed the other and, keeping hold of both, mounted and rode back to Laredo.

The lawman, already sweating in the oppressive heat, dropped his saddle and eyed Will as if he were a stranger. 'They hang horse thieves,' he said flatly.

'I didn't steal him,' Will replied. 'In fact, I'm doing the honorable thing. Since its owner is dead, I'm taking the horse back to town and turning it over to the *rurales*.'

'There ain't no *rurales* in Matamoros,' Laredo said. 'No *rurales*, no *Guardia civil*, no *Federales*! Just one old *ex-pistolero* who only agreed to be a policeman so he could look important in the uniform and get free beer and tortillas in the cantinas.'

'I've always admired free enterprise,' Will said.

Laredo's temper flared. 'You keep

funning around in Matamoros, boy, and you'll find yourself feet-up in a wooden box six feet under!'

'Okay, okay, calm down. I get it. No need to throw a snit!'

'I ain't throwing a snit,' Laredo growled. 'I'm just ... Goddammit, Will, can't you see I'm trying to keep you alive?'

'Sure I can. And I appreciate it, too. I really do.'

'Then will you rope in your joking around?'

'Definitely.'

'Otherwise the riffraff in Matamoros will have the last laugh,' Laredo continued as if Will hadn't responded. 'They'll applaud your joke and then gun you down for your boots.'

'I said 'definitely', didn't I?'

Laredo nodded, but it was obvious he wasn't convinced.

'From now on, you'll see a new me,' Will assured him. 'I'll be so serious you won't recognize me.'

'Good.'

'I do have one tiny little question for you.'

'Shoot.'

'Do you think maybe — just maybe — you're capable of transferring saddles without my illustrious help?'

Laredo rolled his eyes. 'You just can't help it, can you?'

'What, what?'

'Forget it,' Laredo said resignedly. 'Just piss off and let me saddle up.'

'Gladly.' Will wheeled his horse around and gently spurred the roan in the direction of Matamoros.

He hadn't gone more than a mile when Laredo caught up with him.

'Now who's the horse thief?' Will said.

'It ain't stealing when you're a lawman,' Laredo replied.

'No? What is it then?'

'It's called commandeering. You being one of them smart school-taught fellas from Boston — '

'Philadelphia — '

' — Philadelphia, I would've thought

you'd know that.'

'Must've been one of the classes I was too drunk to attend,' Will said. 'But I surely do thank you for enlightening me.'

Laredo grunted in a way that could have meant anything . . . and they rode on.

*   *   *

On reaching the outskirts of Matamoros, Laredo chose not to enter town but rode around behind the old church. He didn't try to encourage or stop Will from accompanying him, and the two men entered the rundown building like silent shadows.

Laredo, anxious to make sure that Father Delgado was safe, led the way through the crumbling ruins to the padre's meager quarters. Before they reached there, they heard murmuring inside the chancel. Laredo put his finger to his lips. Will nodded to show he understood. Keeping as quiet as possible they ducked through an opening in one of the damaged walls, entered the chancel and paused by the altar.

At first glance there seemed to be no one around. But the faint murmuring continued. Laredo thumbed at a small, hand-carved wooden confessional that stood against the far wall. The booth had been damaged and spit upon, like everything else, but there was still enough of it remaining to give privacy to Father Delgado, who sat on one side listening through a lattice to the old white-haired *campesino* facing him.

Laredo and Will took a seat on one of the remaining pews and waited impatiently for the confession to end. When it did, the old *campesino* emerged. Reverently crossing himself, he looked fearfully around as if afraid of being seen, and hurried from the church.

Moments later Father Delgado appeared and confronted Laredo and Will, who respectfully stood up. The old padre looked as dirty and rumpled as ever; and, worse, reeked of whisky.

'P-Please forgive my transgreshuns,' he began.

Laredo cut him off, saying urgently: 'Father, listen to me. Nix is here, in town!'

'I know, *mi hijo*. I shaw him a liddle while ago when he rode in with his m-men.'

'We jumped 'em at Vasquez Rocks,' Will explained, 'and been chasing them ever since.'

'Which is why you must get away from here, *muy pronto*,' Laredo said. 'You know how twisted Nix can get, Father. He might blame you for telling us where he and his men were and come looking for his pound of flesh.'

'Thank you for warning me,' Father Delgado said, 'both of you. But I do not fear Nix or his vengeance. I am an old man who has outlived his usefulness. God is aware of that. If I should die by Nix's hand it is because the Lord intended it that way. Nix is my salvation . . . God's way of cleansing me of my sins and relieving me of my suffering.'

'Now you're talking *loco*,' said Laredo.

'He's right, Father,' added Will. 'Nix is scum. Satan reincarnated. No God, however omnipotent or mysterious, would deal with Carson Nix.'

'I got a horse outside,' Laredo continued. 'If you leave now, Father, we'll make sure you get safely out of town. Then you can either go hide in one of the villages or take the ferry and find sanctuary in the U.S.'

The old padre smiled and shook his head. 'I shall never leave this church, *mi hijo*, no matter what dangers I face or however many men like Nix threaten me.' He paused, reverently blessed Laredo and Will, and said: 'Go now, both of you. Leave me to my prayers.' Turning, he shuffled slowly off to his quarters.

Laredo looked after him, frustrated. 'Priests,' he said disgustedly. 'I swear it's easier to ride 'cross Texas in the dead of winter than to make 'em see reason.'

'They *can* be difficult to figure out,' Will agreed. 'I know. Being an agnostic — '

'You're an agnostic?' Laredo said, surprised.

Will nodded. 'Which, as you can imagine, isn't the easiest subject to discuss with a priest. Any priest.'

'Why try? Your feelings 'bout God or His existence, hell, they're strictly your business.'

'Not according to my dear father. He's a zealot when it comes to religion, and took my lack of faith as a personal attack on his own beliefs. He threatened to cut me off and to even kick me out of the family if I didn't accept God. And when that didn't work, he brought in priests and even the local bishop to try to change my views.'

'How'd that go over?'

'Ugly at best. I mean, by the time they got through with me, I felt like I was Satan being kicked out of heaven.'

'Father Delgado probably has similar feelings,' Laredo said. ''Cept he knows that the only place Nix will kick him is into his grave.'

'You think that's why he's drinking again?'

'Could be.'

'So what're we going to do?'

'Only thing we can do — kill Nix 'fore he can kill Father Delgado or anyone else.'

'Now you're talking! When do we get started?'

'You don't,' Laredo said. 'I'm handling Nix alone.'

'But I thought I was your deputy?'

'*Temporary* deputy. I'm revoking your authority as of now!' Turning, Laredo hurried off.

22

Laredo stared over the batwing doors of *La Rana Purpura* and checked the hard cases drinking along the bar. Neither Nix nor his men were among them. His gaze swept the noisy, smoke-filled room. Several men, whom Laredo recognized from 'Wanted' posters, were playing poker in the corner, while others, equally lawless, sat drinking at tables facing the cantina door.

Laredo pushed inside, trying to watch everyone at once, his right hand on the butt of his holstered six-gun. Everyone gave him unfriendly stares, but when they realized he wasn't there to arrest them they returned to their conversations.

The men at the bar grudgingly stepped aside as he approached, giving him room to talk to the bartender.

Laredo asked the big-bellied, hairy-armed Mexican if he'd seen Carson Nix. The barkeep kept his head down and didn't answer. In an effort to ignore Laredo, he continued to rinse and dry a stack of glasses. Laredo, finally losing his patience, leaned across the bar and grabbed the man by the shirt.

'I asked you a question, mister. You'd do well to answer it.'

'He is not here, *señor*,' the barkeep said sullenly. 'He is maybe 'cross the border somewhere.'

Laredo released the barkeep's shirt and in the same smooth motion drew his Colt, thumbed back the hammer and jammed the barrel into the barkeep's bulging gut.

'You're lying, mister,' he said. 'How do I know that? I've been dogging Nix's trail for almost a week now, and finally caught up with him earlier today at Vasquez Rocks. I almost had him. But he managed to shake me and headed for here. I figured he and the two men with him might have crossed the river by now. But the ferryman swears he never carried them across, and since he's got no reason to lie, I believe him. Which means Nix is here, in beautiful stinking downtown Matamoros, and I aim to find out where. So fill your mouth with words, or I'll fill your belly with lead!'

The barkeep paled and sweat ran down his forehead.

'*Por favor, señor*, I cannot say. *Señor* Nix, he will kill me and my family if I do.'

Laredo, despite empathizing with the barkeep's dilemma, said coldly: 'And I'll kill you if you don't. So it's up to you, *amigo*. Die now or die later. Your call.'

Panic creased the bartender's fat, sweaty face.

'I ain't got all night,' Laredo said when the barkeep kept silent. 'So unless you got a third option I don't know about, I suggest — '

'He does, Marshal,' a voice said behind Laredo. 'Me.'

Laredo swung around and saw Carson Nix standing in the doorway to the kitchen, Colt in one hand and a half-eaten tortilla stuffed with *frijoles* in the other.

'Drop it,' Nix said, indicating the six-gun in Laredo's hand. 'Otherwise you're going to rob me of the pleasure of gutting you neck to gizzard.'

Laredo grudgingly set his Colt on the bar. 'Where're your friends?' he said, stalling. 'Hiding in the kitchen with you?'

'We wasn't hiding,' Nix said. 'We were stuffing our guts while waiting on you.'

'Well, I'm here now,' Laredo said. 'So I reckon the next move's up to you.' Even as he spoke, he grabbed a glass of beer from in front of the man beside him and hurled it at Nix — at the same time diving over the bar.

Nix ducked the thrown glass and fired at Laredo. His bullet missed and splintered the bar top, ricocheted and shattered the big mirror behind the bar. Shards of broken glass flew everywhere, forcing everyone to duck.

Taking advantage of the chaos, Laredo grabbed the shotgun the barkeep kept under the bar and fired both barrels at Nix. But the outlaw, anticipating Laredo's move, was already diving for cover, and the buckshot chewed a chunk out of the door.

Nix's men, who'd been eating in the kitchen, dropped to the floor and crawled to the damaged door. There, guns in hand, they opened fire at Laredo, forcing him to again duck below the bar.

By now everyone else in the cantina had taken cover behind overturned tables and chairs. From here they watched as Laredo exchanged shots with Nix and his two men.

'Looks like what we got here,' Nix said as he reloaded, 'is one of them Mexican standoffs, wouldn't you say, Marshal?'

'Looks like,' Laredo agreed. 'Only difference is, my deputy's already on his way to Brownsville for help.'

'What help?' Nix scoffed. 'The law ain't worth dog piss down here. This is Mexico, remember?'

'Who said anything 'bout the law?' Laredo replied. 'Fellas he's rounding up are Texicans — men tired of dealing with outlaws and rustlers, men willing to risk their lives to build a better and safer Texas!'

Nix laughed unpleasantly. 'Sounds like you're running for office, Marshal.' Then, as his men joined in laughing: 'You hear that, boys? Mr. Marshal here is threatening to bring the wrath of Texas down upon us if we don't throw down our guns.'

'I'll go to hell first,' replied one of the men.

'Yeah,' said the other, 'and we'll take him 'long with us.'

'Sorry, Marshal,' Nix told Laredo. 'Seems like my boys ain't interested in your offer.'

'Then they'll have to pay the price,' Laredo said. 'And so will you.' About to open fire, he saw someone familiar enter the cantina, and immediately lowered his Colt.

'Get out of here, Father!' he yelled to the old padre. 'You'll get yourself killed!'

Father Delgado ignored him and slowly walked toward Nix. His cowl was pulled over his head, hiding his face, and he walked unsteadily, obviously under the influence of the whisky bottle poking from his robe pocket.

'Father . . . Father, please,' Laredo begged. 'Don't do this — '

His plea was drowned out by gunfire.

Laredo winced, expecting to see Father Delgado crumple to the floor.

Instead, flame belched from the padre's robe and one of Nix's men crouched by the door collapsed on his face. The other cursed and swung around to shoot Father Delgado. Before he could, Laredo shot him in the chest, sending him sprawling.

Nix, realizing he was now alone, took a quick shot at Laredo, missed and ran into the kitchen.

Father Delgado fired after him, but also missed.

Laredo scrambled over the bar, intent on pursuing Nix. But as he drew abreast of Father Delgado, the old padre pushed his cowl back, revealing his face.

Laredo gaped at him. 'Y-You!'

Will grinned. 'Told you I wasn't going to run out on you, partner.'

Laredo was momentarily lost for words. 'W-Where's Father Delgado?' he finally asked.

'Enjoying a siesta.' Will took the whisky bottle from his pocket and held it up to show it was empty. 'Happily, I might add.'

Laredo shook his head in amazement. Then: 'C'mon!' he yelled. 'The sonofabitch is getting away!' He ran into the kitchen, followed closely by Will.

23

As the two of them ran through the kitchen, scattering pots and pans hanging in their way, they heard a horse galloping away outside. They burst out the door and saw Nix astride his big leggy gray, riding toward the river. The ferry dock was only a short distance beyond him. It was crowded with men, women and families all boarding to be taken across to the U.S., and as Will raised his gun to shoot Nix, Laredo pulled his arm down, saying: 'Let him go.'

'But it might take weeks, even months to track him down.'

'So be it.'

'*So be it*? What the hell kind of answer is that?'

'A wise one,' Laredo said. He thumbed at the crowded ferry. 'It's too risky. Even if you did hit Nix, you might just wing him, and then the bullet could ricochet and kill someone else, like mine did. You want that on your conscience?'

'I guess not ... ' Will grudgingly lifted the robe and holstered his Colt, watching, frustrated, as Nix led his horse onto the ferry. The ferryman made sure everyone was safely aboard the rowboats, then untied the barge and signaled to the men on the rope across the river to start pulling.

Standing at the stern, Nix gave a mocking wave to Laredo.

Will gave a grumbling sigh and removed Father Delgado's old tattered robe. 'You might be right after all,' he said, throwing the robe on the trash piled outside the back door of the cantina. 'Maybe I'm not cut out to be a lawman.'

'What're you talking about?' Laredo exclaimed.

'Well, you have to be patient and wise, like you are, and — '

'Patience be damned,' Laredo broke

in. 'Disguising yourself as Father Delgado? Judas, *hombre*, that was one of the slickest tricks I've ever seen.'

'Really?'

'Really.'

'*Serious*?'

'Serious.'

'Yeah,' Will admitted after he'd thought about it, 'come to think of it, it was pretty slick.'

'Right up there at the top of the totem pole,' Laredo said.

'At the top, huh?'

'Very top.'

'Damn,' Will said smugly. 'Imagine that? I mean, just think. One day, years from now, kids in schools in Philly will read all about this — you know, how I saved your life? — in their history books. And then, you know what, they'll think I was one of the smartest lawmen who ever lived — smarter even than Bat Masterson or Wyatt Earp!'

Laredo rolled his eyes. 'God help me,' he muttered. 'I've created a monster.'

24

It was almost a half-hour later when they led their horses off the barge onto U.S. soil, swung up into the saddle and rode into Brownsville.

'Where do you think we should look first?' Will asked as they followed a freight wagon into town. 'I know the Empire is Nix's favorite watering hole, but surely he wouldn't be so stupid as not to think that's the first place we'd look for him?'

Laredo shrugged. 'Sometimes the obvious is the safest place to hide. Hold your horses,' he added as Will started to interrupt, 'I ain't finished.'

'Sorry. Go on.'

'However, knowing we're right on his heels, I reckon Nix will stay clear of the Empire — 'least for a while, anyway — and hole up someplace less conspicuous.'

'Like where?'

'Sure you want to know?'

'Dammit, don't play games. 'Course I want to know.'

'Then stick close to me,' Laredo said, 'and watch and listen.' He nudged his horse on around the next corner, and followed the side-street to the end where opposite Whalen's Livery Stable was a plain two-story wooden building.

'Whoa,' exclaimed Will, reining up. 'I know this place.'

'You ought to,' Laredo said. 'It's where I almost killed you.'

'Kate's Place!' Will's hand strayed to the scab-covered scar formed on his temple by Laredo's bullet. 'A whorehouse?' he then said questioningly. 'You honestly think at a time like this, Nix is going to risk his life for a roll in the hay?'

'Not just any roll in the hay,' Laredo said. ''Cording to a friend of mine, an old busybody who lives with her ear to the ground and an eye at the keyhole, Nix is so sweet on this one young whore, he can't stay away from her. But you already know that, 'cause you reminded me about it on the ride up here. Said that's why Nix was headed here in the first place.'

'I did, didn't I?' Will said. 'Huh. I'm even smarter than I thought. Just joking,' he added quickly as Laredo glared at him. 'Don't throw a shoe.'

Laredo clenched his teeth. 'If you're all done funning around, maybe we can get back to finding Nix.'

'Lead the way,' Will said cheerfully. 'But once we get inside Kate's, don't go mistaking me for Nix again. I don't need any more of your lead digging holes in my head!'

'Then keep behind me,' Laredo said. 'Or better still, go wait for me in the Empire. When I'm done with Nix, I'll join you, and we can both celebrate by bending a few elbows together.'

Will stared at Laredo, unable to believe his gall.

'All right, all right,' Laredo said. 'Maybe that wasn't such a good idea.

You've earned the right to be in on this. Just — '

'Keep behind you,' finished Will. 'Yeah, yeah, I get it, Marshal. In other words, do as I'm told and watch your back?'

Laredo, hearing the disgust in Will's voice, turned and gripped the young man by both shoulders.

'Listen,' he said quietly, 'I know I've been tough on you. And coming from me, this probably won't mean much to you. But the truth is, Deputy Willard Bronson, there ain't nobody I'd sooner have protecting my back than you.'

He sounded sincere but Will didn't trust him. 'All right,' he demanded suspiciously. 'What's going on?'

'What do you mean?'

'You just gave me a compliment. 'Least, it sounded like a compliment. Yes,' he said as if convincing himself, 'it definitely was a compliment all right.'

'So?'

'So why now?'

'I told you. You earned it.'

'Really?'

Laredo scowled. 'Now don't start repeating 'really' again or I'll take it back.'

'Too late. You can't take a compliment back.'

'Watch me.'

'No, no, no. You don't understand. Compliments are like insults. Once you say them, they're out there permanently, floating around for all the world to see. Doesn't matter how much you regret saying it either, because — ' He broke off as he suddenly felt the barrel of Laredo's Colt jammed against his neck.

'One more word — no, one more *sound* — out of you,' Laredo said sweetly, 'and I'll blow your goddamn Adam's apple clean out of your throat! Clear?'

Will nodded very, very slowly, eyes bugged, not even daring to breathe.

'*Bueno.*' Laredo returned the Colt to its holster. 'Now, let's get this over with.' Dismounting, he led Will around to the rear door. Two horses were tied up there. Neither belonged to Nix.

'He's probably stabled the gray 'cross the street,' Laredo said.

'Doesn't Mr. Whalen know Nix is an outlaw?'

'Sure. But he ain't fool enough tell him he can't stable his horse there. Knows he'd be eating dirt if he did.' Easing open the door, Laredo beckoned for Will to follow him. The two of them crept along the narrow hallway to the stairs leading up to the second floor.

'Want me to check the rooms down here?' Will whispered as they reached the foot of the stairs.

Laredo shook his head. 'All the action's upstairs. What you *can* do, though, is stay here and make sure Nix don't somehow sneak past me. Don't look like that,' he said as Will scowled. 'I ain't trying to protect you — fact is, I'm counting on you to protect someone else.'

'Who?'

'Kate. She's an old friend of mine,

and if Nix does get by me, he'll be so pissed that I busted up his daily hump, he might take his anger out on her. And that wouldn't be pretty.'

'Don't worry,' Will promised. 'If Nix shows, I'll see to it the SOB never leaves these stairs.'

Laredo brushed past him and crept up the stairs, gun in hand, straining to identify the voices and laughter coming from the various bedrooms. Nix's voice wasn't among them. Laredo reached the top of the stairs and paused, again listening intently to the grunts, moans and squeals of pleasure happening all around him.

Still no Nix. Frustrated, he was about to start along the dimly-lit hall when he heard Nix's cruel laughter. It came from the end bedroom. Laredo froze. Listened again. This time he heard the woman with Nix giggling. Then, suddenly, there was the sound of a slap, followed not by a scream but a squeal of sexual pleasure. Another slap followed, harder and more vicious. The woman cried out, this time not from pleasure but from pain and fear. A third, even harder slap followed, and suddenly the woman screamed and begged Nix to stop.

Laredo used the screaming to hide his footsteps as he hurried along the hall to the end bedroom. Inside, he could hear Nix cursing the woman as she sobbed and pleaded for him to stop.

Laredo thumbed back the hammer of his Colt and kicked the door in.

The sight before him sickened and enraged him. There on the bed kneeled Nix, naked save for his boots and his gun-belt, a young, dark-haired whore pinned on her back by his knees. Her once-pretty face was puffy and bruised from his blows. Blood ran from her mouth, her lips were split and one eye was swollen shut.

Nix, in the middle of delivering another blow, whirled and saw Laredo facing him, ready to shoot.

There was no mercy in Laredo's eyes and Nix knew better than to expect any.

He grabbed for his gun.

Fast as he was — and he *was* fast — he couldn't beat Laredo's trigger finger.

Laredo fired once, the .45 slug punching a hole right between Nix's squinted eyes.

Nix fell back, dead but somehow not accepting the fact, his gun-hand still clawing at his Colt.

Laredo shot him again, this time in the heart. The outlaw flopped backward and sideways, his body sliding off the petrified young whore onto the floor. He lay there in a motionless heap, blood pouring from the gaping hole in the back of his head.

Laredo stepped closer, peering down at Nix to make sure he was dead.

It was a mistake. He wasn't watching the whore, who lunged for a derringer resting on a table beside the bed.

Laredo whirled — but knew even as he did that he was too late to stop her from killing him.

It was then another shot was fired. It

came from behind him. The bullet struck the young whore in the throat. Her bubbling cry was choked off, and even as Laredo turned to see who had fired, the young whore collapsed on the bed.

'Shame on you,' Kate said from the doorway. 'I taught you better than that, L.J.'

''Never turn your back on a woman',' he said, quoting.

'Especially when you've just shot her lover.'

Laredo ruefully shook his head. 'Just goes to show you, don't it? You ain't never too old to learn.'

'I'm glad to hear you admit that,' Will said, joining Kate in the doorway. ''Cause I'm going to keep reminding you of it every time you start acting like you're perfect!'

Laredo looked at Kate and rolled his eyes.

'Do me one small favor,' he begged her. 'Shoot the sonofabitch while you got the chance!'

25

It was nearing midday and the Texas sun was at full broil when Laredo and Will rode up to the main gate of Huntsville Prison. Dripping sweat, they reined their horses in and sat there in grim silence.

'You sure you want to do this?' Will said. 'I mean, it's not too late to change your mind.'

'In other words, break my word?'

'That's one way of looking at it, I suppose.'

'Tell me another?'

'Well . . . this woman — what's her name?'

'Miriam Hargrove.'

' — Hargrove, she probably doesn't know Nix is dead yet. I mean, you haven't told her and I certainly haven't — '

'But Marshal Macahan has.'

'You don't know that. Not for sure. Hell, Brownsville might not have notified him, or — or maybe he's not in El Paso right now. Maybe he's off hunting down outlaws and — '

'This ain't about Macahan,' Laredo broke in. 'It ain't even 'bout the law.'

'It isn't?'

'Uh-uh.'

'What, then?'

Laredo sighed and shifted uncomfortably in his saddle. 'If I got to tell you, son, then all the days and nights we've spent together have been a pure waste of time.'

'Maybe to you, but not to me,' Will said. 'I mean, I haven't always agreed with what you've said or done, and I sure haven't always liked how you told me, but at the same time I've learned a lot from you — a hell of a lot!'

'Name something.'

'Lying, for starters.'

'Lying? Hell, I never lied to you about nothing!'

'Oh, no? What about the reward

money for Nix that never existed?'

'I never said it did. I simply said, whatever reward there was, it was all yourn.'

Unable to deny that, Will said grudgingly: 'Maybe you're right. Anyway, I learned a lot more than lies.'

'Like, what?'

''Bout being a man.'

'Go on.'

'And being responsible.'

'They're one and the same.'

'So I've learned, thanks to you.' Will paused as the prison gate opened with a loud clank and two armed uniformed guards stepped out into the bright sunlight. 'Now it's too late,' he said glumly.

Laredo eyed the approaching guards. They wagged their rifles at him, indicating for him to get off his horse. Laredo nodded to show he understood and then slowly, carefully unbuckled his gun-belt.

'Here,' he said, handing it to Will. 'Look after this for me, will you?'

'S-Sure. But why me?'

''Cause I'm going to need it again one day. And when I do I want to be sure it's oiled, cleaned and waiting for me.'

Will took the gun-belt, eyes watering for a moment. 'Count on it,' he said. 'Partner.'

'I am,' Laredo said. He dismounted and handed Will the reins. 'Just like I'm counting on you to be my deputy again next time Hargrove needs me to kill another outlaw. Partner.'

For a long moment the two friends locked gazes. Then Laredo turned and walked toward the guards.

Will watched as the guards fastened wrist- and leg-irons on Laredo and escorted him into the prison.

'Hey, *hombre* — '

Laredo looked back over his shoulder. 'Yeah?'

'Is it okay if I sell your horse and saddle? There's this pretty little whore at Kate's Place ... ' He burst out laughing, unable to finish.

Laredo scowled at him for another moment, then realized Will was joking and ruefully shook his head. Facing front, he continued shuffling along between the guards, leg-irons jingling, into the prison. The heavy barred-gate slammed behind them with a loud and foreboding clank.

Will's laughter subsided. He wiped the tears from his eyes with his knuckle and sighed, heavy-hearted, knowing he'd just lost the first true friend he'd ever had. And maybe would ever have.

'Damn,' he said softly. 'Damn, damn, damn.' Then he wheeled his horse around, tapped his heels against its flanks, and the red roan obediently loped away.

We do hope that you have enjoyed reading this large print book.

Did you know that all of our titles are available for purchase?

We publish a wide range of high quality large print books including:
Romances, Mysteries, Classics
General Fiction
Non Fiction and Westerns

Special interest titles available in large print are:
The Little Oxford Dictionary
Music Book, Song Book
Hymn Book, Service Book

Also available from us courtesy of Oxford University Press:
Young Readers' Dictionary
(large print edition)
Young Readers' Thesaurus
(large print edition)

For further information or a free brochure, please contact us at:
Ulverscroft Large Print Books Ltd.,
The Green, Bradgate Road, Anstey,
Leicester, LE7 7FU, England.
Tel: (00 44) **0116 236 4325**
Fax: (00 44) **0116 234 0205**

Other titles in the
Linford Western Library:

BADMAN SHERIFF

Simon Webb

When the citizens of Coopers Creek elect Ned Turner as their sheriff, they are blind to the deadly mistake being made. For Turner is a lawless rogue seeking to exploit the position for his own advantage. It will be left to mild-mannered baker Jack Crawley to set things right. But can he rescue his town from the worst badman sheriff Montana has ever known?

LEGEND OF THE DEAD MEN'S GOLD

I. J. Parnham

Ten years ago, the Helliton gang holed up in a stronghold with a stolen wagonload of gold. One year later, all of them were dead — fallen defending their hoard from other outlaws, and fighting amongst themselves. The last living gang member cursed the gold, saying that if he couldn't have it, nobody would. Or so the legend goes . . . Trip Kincaid had always been fascinated by the tale. His brother Oliver suspects it's the true reason behind his sudden disappearance — and is determined to find him . . .

SAM AND THE SHERIFF

Billy Hall

Sheriff Ned Garman patrols his juris-
diction with Justus, his horse of many
colors, and Sam, his loyal and shaggy
dog. Together, the three make a perfect team. When a herder from Lars
Ingevold's sheep ranch is gunned down,
Garman is straight on the trail of the
culprit, and concludes that the killer
tried to implicate the Shoshone Indi-
ans in the crime. But Ingevold, constantly
squabbling with the neighbouring cattle
ranch over grazing rights, suspects
the I Bar W is responsible. It seems
that somebody's aiming to spark a
range war . . .

TROUBLE AT NATHAN'S FORD

Jack Sheriff

When a night bank robbery in Drystone City goes horribly wrong, Cage turns his back on lawlessness and heads home. But when he arrives in the border town of Nathan's Ford, he rides into tragedy: his father's ranch has been burned to the ground, killing his parents, and his brother is on the run. And there's even worse news: the Drystone bank owner has ridden into town, armed to the teeth — seeking to avenge the death of his wife at the hands of the robbers . . .

THE GOLD BONANZA

John Russell Fearn

Loping along the trail, old prospector Dusty Morgan literally falls headlong into a bonanza — a lost Aztec gold-mine. Desperate to share the news of his good fortune, despite knowing he should keep quiet, he confides in saloon girl Val Kent. But can she be trusted? And there are other eyes watching and other ears listening: saloon owner Drew Carson and his unscrupulous gunhawk. Meanwhile, a ruthless Aztec woman, Maninza, regards the gold as her rightful ancestral property . . .